The Disappeared
MONEY

by

ED STAUFFER

ISBN 978-1-956001-53-2 (paperback)
ISBN 978-1-956001-54-9 (eBook)

Printed in the United States of America

Chapter 1

There wasn't much traffic early on Wednesday morning. It was dark because the sun hadn't risen yet as the taxi raced along toward the Reagan Airport, and since there was little traffic, the taxi made good time. It was warm but would get warmer as the day started and the sun rose. The east coast was experiencing an abnormal warm spell for early October. The temperature would rise into the low to mid-seventies and soon the city would begin a new day. Traffic picked up as the taxi neared the airport. The driver had asked which airline when Detective Marcus Rothman entered the cab and he said United. He was fit, in his early thirties, fourth year detective with the San Francisco police. He had left his service gun at home because he would be going through security check points. He could have gotten a TSA security permit but decided against it. He wouldn't need it. He was not in Washington on official police business but rather attending a police sensitivity workshop that his chief ordered him to attend, and then bring back the important information and set up several classes in his own department. The detective was opposed to the trip. Why him? He had never had a complaint from a citizen. But his chief was insistent, so here he was.

Once the taxi began to move the driver asked if he had been to Washington for business or pleasure. Marcus thought about it and waited a moment before answering the driver, since he was busy the entire time, he said business and didn't explain. He was scheduled to leave tomorrow but called the airline and changed his ticket when the workshop ended a day early. Downside of leaving a day early was the very early morning flight. If he wished to change his ticket it was the only flight with an available seat unless he wished to fly stand by. No way was he going to wait around the airport hoping someone would cancel their flight. Better to be in his hometown, San Francisco, for the long weekend that he would have ahead of him. He believed that he could sleep on the plane. For the remainder of the ride neither he nor the driver said anything.

When the taxi pulled up to the United Airlines terminal and stopped, the driver told Marcus the trip cost him thirty-four forty. He took out his wallet, removed his credit card and prepared to swipe it when he asked the driver if he could add a fifteen percent tip, the only amount the department would reimburse him for. The driver said yes and told Marcus to swipe his card. He followed the driver's request and swiped his card. "Follow the instructions," the driver said. Marcus tapped tip and various percentages showed up. He tapped the fifteen percent, then tapped the green finished. The driver thanked him as the receipt was printed and he handed it to Marcus. He folded the receipt and put it in his pocket. The driver got out, opened the taxi's trunk and retrieved Marcus' suitcase. The taxi driver placed the suitcase on the sidewalk and because Marcus never told the taxi driver what he did for a living, he addressed the detective as sir, and wished the detective a safe flight.

In the airport, Marcus got into the check-in line, proceeded to the counter, got his boarding pass, and checked his suitcase. It took him about half an hour to get through the TSA and then to the airline waiting area. His flight didn't depart for an hour, so he went to a nearby Starbucks kiosk, bought a coffee and a cinnamon roll, returned to the waiting area, and finished off both. He sat back in his seat and must have dozed off because the next thing he heard was an airline announcement. When he opened his eyes, he saw the waiting area was crowded and people were lined up at the door to the airplane. He heard first class and people that needed assistance or were with children allowed to board the plane. He saw no children or people needing assistance. He waited for people to board. He was in no hurry and had nothing that would need to be stored overhead and knew the plane wouldn't leave until everyone was boarded. If he ever met an airline person he was going to ask, why is it that the people in the front of the plane are asked to board first so that they created a bottle neck, people trying to get around them. Like a lot of things, he wondered about, he most likely would not follow through on it.

Finally, he was on the plane, looked at his ticket and began to look for his seat and found it. It was a window seat in the last row on the left side of the plane. He couldn't complain because it was the only seat available if he wanted to change his ticket. He took off his sports coat and folded it, excused himself as he squeezed past the man sitting on the aisle. Only two seats in this row. This early in the morning he thought it a little strange, he could smell alcohol on his traveling companion. Maybe the guy needed a shot of courage in the morning to get started. He preferred coffee. Once he was in his seat, he settled in, fastened his seat belt, held his coat on his lap and closed his eyes as a stewardess announced that seat belts should be fastened and trays in their upright position. He could hear her as she demonstrated how to fasten the seat belt and how to use the oxygen mask if needed. That done she began to tell about the safety features of the plane, the emergency exits were pointed out, and that the bottom seat cushion could be used as a floatation device if the plane were to land in the water. Turn off all electronic devices until after the plane is air born and make sure all carry-ons are safely stored. He turned off the overhead light, closed his eyes and could feel the plane move as it began to taxi out to the runway. The next thing he heard was the pilot telling the flight crew to take their seats. He believed that the plane had taxied a long time before it got into its take off pattern. Maybe it was his imagination. The pilot came on the intercom and announced that they were returning to the loading gate to fix a problem with the plane. That got his attention as well as that of a few other passengers and grumbling could be heard. He turned on his overhead light and waited.

When the plane reached the loading gate the pilot came on the intercom again and told everyone not to worry. The problem was a light that was not on and would have to be replaced. It shouldn't take long and that everyone should be patient. The plane's crew would be serving drinks while the light was being replaced.

The man sitting beside Marcus finally said, "Seems like we've been sitting here for over an hour and it's hot in here. Christ, the sun is coming up!"

Marcus turned and stared out his window and could see the sky showed where the sun would soon rise. He looked at his watch, shook his head no and replied, "Less than twenty minutes," he said to the man sitting beside him and said, "You have your sports coat on, that's why it's warm. Take it off like I did."

"Seemed like an hour, and policy says we must always maintain proper dress code, and a sports coat is considered proper dress," Detective Marcus Rothman's traveling companion said.

"Aren't you hot with your jacket on? Who is going to know?" he asked. Before Marcus' companion could answer, the stewardess could be seen pushing her cart toward them, she was just ahead of their row, then she was at their row, and Marcus's traveling companion's attention turned to the stewardess. She served the two passengers across the aisle first. The passenger said, "Bout time you got here. Samantha, that your name? Says it on your name tag," he said to her. She replied it was her name and what could she get him to drink. The words were just out of her mouth when he said, "Bring me a scotch and one for my friend here. Two waters."

Samantha didn't know if the bar was open and it was awfully early to be drinking. The passenger insisted it wasn't too early and looked like he could make a scene. "It's the least the airline could do making us wait in a," and he stressed the words, "hot plane." She stepped on the cart's brake, turned, and walked up the aisle.

Marcus looked at the man sitting beside him and commented on his drinking so early and said, "For sure, I don't want a drink."

The man said, "I figured you didn't, but I wanted two. Need two! I knew she wouldn't serve me two. She comes back I'll get you whatever you'd like. Name's Beale, Franklin Beale."

"The water is fine," replied Marcus as he put out his hand to shake Beale's. "My name is Marcus Rothman."

Marcus could detect the nervousness in Franklin Beale's voice when Franklin asked, "How fucking long does it take to change a damn light bulb anyway!?"

"Well," said Marcus, "I'll explain it to you. First it takes time to wrestle up a union crew, wait until their coffee break is over, find the bulb, find a ladder, find a different union crew to hold the ladder only to discover it's the wrong bulb. Then start all over."

Marcus's explanation elicited a chuckle from Beale who said in a more relaxed voice, "Or it's a government job! They are all sitting in an office drinking coffee and planning how it should be done and who is responsible, fill out the paperwork and send it off to the agency responsible to fix it."

The stewardess returned, set the drinks and water on each on the two trays and said, "That will be ten dollars sir. Exact amount or a credit card."

"Should be fucking free making us wait here!" he mumbled as he fished out his wallet and took a ten-dollar bill from it and handed it to the stewardess. She thanked him and started to pull her cart toward the front of the plane. He opened one of the small bottles of scotch and drained it in one big gulp. "That's better," he uttered. He turned and faced Marcus and said, "No, it's not too early, I don't like to fly. This helps, settles me down, makes the trip bearable and gives me courage."

Beale unscrewed the lid of the second bottle but before he could take a drink Marcus asked, "You an air marshal of some sort and afraid to fly?"

Beale drank half of the second bottle and asked, "What makes you think that?"

"I see you are armed and probably the reason for not removing your sports coat. You must be an official of some sort to get past TSA. Or you are a high jacker and somehow got past the screening and got on board."

Beale put the half bottle of scotch down and smiled as he looked at Marcus. "I'm an armed government agent escort. To Frisco and then on to Asia. How'd you know I am armed?"

Now it was Marcus' turn to smile when he answered, "Trained to spot things like that. I'm a police detective out of San Francisco. Here in DC for police sensitivity training that I will be able to take back and work with some of my guys. I didn't see anyone on my way to here in the back of the plane that would need escorted or guarded and it sure ain't me."

"I asked to be seated in the rear of the plane, read one time it is the safest place to be if the plane should crash." Beale paused and then continued, "It's not in the plane. What I'm escorting is in cargo. I work for the treasury department. Without telling you what it is let me say if we crash in water, rent some scuba gear. It would last for years."

Marcus said, "Unlikely we will crash in water, not much between here and California. We'd most likely come down on land, maybe in a corn field, a forest or in the mountains."

"In that case," Beale replied, "get yourself a good pair of hiking boots." He finished his scotch and took a drink of water. He looked at Marcus and asked, "What if I were a terrorist. I wanted to hijack the plane, pulled my gun?"

"I'd have put you down, period!" replied Marcus.

"What about my partner up front?" Beale asked.

"Well, I'd have taken your gun and we'd have had a shoot-out. I'm a good shot. One of us would have been killed," Marcus said matter-of-factly.

"You're okay," Beale said. He looked up and saw Samantha walking down the aisle with her plastic bag collecting trash, motioned to her, and said, "Two more drinks here."

Marcus said loud enough for Samantha to hear, "No thanks, I have a rule about two drinks before sun-up."

Samantha said to Beale, "Sorry sir. We are about to taxi to the runway. The bar is closed. Give me your trash and make sure your trays are up."

She returned toward the front of the plane and Beale said, "Nice ass. How's the airline able to find so many good-looking women? Wonder if I asked her out, she would accept and see me on my return trip?"

"Beats me," Marcus said and the two of them saw her return to her seat behind and to the right of them. It was true what the treasury agent said about the stewardess. She was a pretty, well-built shapely blonde and most likely in her early thirties or late twenties. He thought she could be a movie star. He didn't see a ring on her finger but today that didn't mean anything. Marcus thought she could be married and as attractive as she was, surely had a boyfriend. In a lowered voice, Marcus told him, "Why don't you ask her and find out?" Beale didn't reply.

Again, Marcus heard the announcement about tray tables up, electronic devices off and all carry-ons stored. He pulled the window shade down, turned his overhead light off and leaned back and closed his eyes. He had no idea how long he may have slept. An announcement over the plane's intercom awakened him. He heard the pilot say, "Please take your seats and fasten your seat belts. We are approaching some turbulent weather. I am going to try and fly around and go above it." Now that he was awake, he felt cold. Marcus loosened his seat belt, leaned forward as far as possible and put his sport coat on. He leaned back, closed his eyes and tried to fall asleep. After a moment Samantha was tapping him on the shoulder and told him to make sure his seat belt was firmly fastened.

Moments later the plane began to rock back and forth, and he could feel it shudder as the plane encountered the bad weather. He lifted the window shade and looked out. All he could see was clouds. He was sure that clouds were not dark gray and black, especially when the plane was this close to them. He tried to look forward as far as he could see through the small window. He saw that what he had seen was not dark clouds, but dark smoke and it was coming from the engine on this side of the plane. It was on fire.

Again, the pilot came on the intercom and made an announcement. He addressed the passengers as ladies and gentlemen and tried to assure them when he said, "The plane has lost an engine on our port side. I've shut it down and the plane is more than capable of flying on one engine. There is nothing to worry about. Everyone should remain seated with their seat belts fastened. I am going to fly lower and the weather was going to make for a rough ride. Flight attendants should take their seats and fasten themselves in." A sudden down draft caused a quick short-lived downward drop of the plane and a momentary feeling of weightlessness. Marcus could again feel the plane rock and looking down at the arm rests he could see Franklin Beale's hand squeezing on it and when he looked at Beale, he could see that he was pale as a sheet. Marcus was tempted to hold his hand and then thought better of it less it be misconstrued. Sensitivity training did not address this sort of a situation, thought that maybe he should have, but he didn't.

Marcus found it difficult to do anything other than try to deal with the rough ride. He thought that he could hear someone in front of him throwing up. Less than five minutes had passed when an explosion was heard, and the plane shook violently. Over the intercom, Marcus heard the pilot announce, "The remaining engine had just exploded and everyone should prepare for a crash landing. Seat belts should be fastened tightly, and everyone should bend forward as far as possible with their heads between their knees. Please follow the flight crew's instructions." Marcus was sure he could hear people throwing up, he could hear others crying and praying. He knew that he was going to die and there was nothing that he could do about it. He was not a very religious man, but he prayed for a moment and told God he was sorry for all the wrong he may have done in his life. Nothing special stood out in his mind as being especially sinful or he needed forgiveness for unless he considered the time with Donna Jean. He remembered, she said he was breaking her heart and she cried, but she was the one who left him. He could hear Beale mumbling but was not sure what he was saying. Was he praying?

The plane was going down in the rough weather the pilot had mentioned, a very bad snowstorm in the mountains of Colorado. As the plane started its descent, its air speed was over three hundred miles per hour. Because of the bad snowstorm and the wind, the pilot had a difficult time controlling the plane, but he was able to keep it level. He could not see where or what the plane would hit, but it was not going to be good. He was sure just like Marcus was, that he and all the passengers and crew were going to die. The altimeter, when the pilot looked at it, was of no use because of the mountains. He told the co-pilot, wheels up, and hoped beyond hope that when the belly of the plane hit, it would slide on the snow. He braced himself for impact and seconds before the plane was to crash, there was a lull in the snowstorm so that the pilot could see what looked like a clearing with few trees, a mountain pasture and from the air it looked level. If he would have only been two miles further to the south, he would have been over about a five square mile lake, and maybe, like the pilot of the plane that landed in New York City's Hudson River, he could have tried to make a water landing. Keeping the nose up, the plane hit at over two hundred miles per hour and began to slide forward. There was nothing the pilot could do. The plane could neither be steered, nor the brakes be applied since the wheels were up. For a second the pilot believed that everyone might survive the crash. But within that second, the port wing hit a medium size tree and instead of breaking off, it bent downward so that it lifted the left wing skyward as the plane's wing cleared a rock out-cropping. Before the tree could swing back, it broke off. The wing on the opposite side of the plane dipped close to the earth and it also hit a tree, a large tree. Instead of bending, tearing the tree in half or even ripping the wing off, all three scenarios could/ should have happened, the tree acted as a pivot point so that the plane spun around on its belly. As fate would have it, the port wing only grazed the large rock out-cropping, but when it spun, the fuselage of the plane hit the rock with such force that behind the wing, the fuselage literally tore in half at the point of impact. The smaller tail half of the plane continued after it bounced off the rock for another thirty yards traveling on its bottom. As it traveled the horizontal stabilizer on the port side tail hit something covered by the snow and was ripped off and the tail section was tipped over onto its side and continued to slide for twenty additional yards before it stopped. Passengers sitting in the seats on the left side of the plane, if they looked out of their windows, all that they would have been able to see was snow pushed up against the windows.

The front half of the plane was not so fortunate. As the fuselage continued to pivot, the part that hit the rock out-cropping was crushed and most likely all the passenger seated in that area were killed. The pivoting fuselage continued its turning until the starboard wing hit the same rock out-cropping. The engine exploded into a ball of flame that soon completely engulfed the front half of the plane.

Not familiar with the make-up or workings of aircraft, Marcus didn't think about it, it just was something that he knew, he was alive and needed to get out of the plane. He unbuckled his seat belt, knew that he would have to climb over the seat to his right, the seat Beale occupied. If Beale would not move Marcus knew he would have to force him out of his seat. He gave it no thought; he just knew what had to be done and he acted. When he turned to his right he found the seat empty, Beale was already gone. He pulled himself up and was able to step onto the arm rest of Beale's seat and he had to stoop so that he wouldn't hit his head on the row of seats that were no longer to his right but above him. The seat didn't have a side and the arm was thin but he could manage to stand up. He was met by the stewardess, Samantha, who was having a difficult time staying erect. She asked for help, not for her, but for other passengers. She told him it would be impossible to open the rear exit escape door and deploy the escape chute. Even if that were possible, how would people be able to climb to it? Their only way out was through the front of the plane and she pointed to the torn opening. Marcus took in all that she said, turned and headed forward. He wondered how she could seem so composed and calm considering the condition they were in.

He had to step around and over passengers trying to get out of their seats and all the overhead items that had fallen from the overhead bins that had broken opened. When he was three seats from the opening, a woman fell from a seat that was now overhead onto the seats across from her that were now below her. She lay there moaning, half on top of the passenger in the seat. Marcus tried to help her up and she moaned more. The man she was partly on lifted her and Marcus pulled her up and heard more groaning. When he had her stooped on the arm rest, he was able to see that her left arm was at an angle, it looked broken. It must have happened when she fell. He held her right arm and urged her forward as he held onto the seat rests above him. The passenger she fell onto had gotten up and out of his seat and he helped support her with his arm around her waist as all three moved forward. The passengers who were in the seats at the break had gotten out. He stepped around the woman he had been helping and was sure the woman was still too high from the snow-covered ground for her to jump. He stepped into the seats kicking the arm rests out of the way until he was standing on the window in a stooped and slanted position. The woman fell to him and he caught her, heard her groan, and turned her to face the opening. She wouldn't have to jump, the tail rested on its side in the snow. He had her step out into the snow. He became aware of the bad snowstorm when he was hit in the face with blowing snow as he told those out of the plane to move away from it.

Before he turned and headed back into the plane's tail, he bent down any sharp metal of the tear that he could see. He helped passenger get out of their seats and stand as best that they could on the arm rests and move forward. Those on the right side of the plane were now overhead and were having problems with unfastening their seat belts and then falling to the row below them. He told them to wait, he'd help them. The overhead bins on the port side had been crunched when the tail slid. He had to force a woman away from trying to open one. Before he reached the rear of the plane he saw several men following his lead and helping fellow passengers out. He could move aside to allow others to get around him. He had to catch seven more passengers when they dropped from above him and had to help an eighth man get up when he fell onto a ninth woman after both released their seat belts. A tenth, another woman, had to be pulled away from trying to open what he assumed was her overhead bin. Marcus could see this side of the plane had crumpled metal and he assumed the bins were crunched closed, couldn't be opened and he shouted the fact to the woman as he pulled her into an upright position.

He eventually reached the rear of the plane where he saw the stewardess, Samantha, having a difficult time with a man above her. Either he couldn't release his seat buckle or was afraid of falling. Marcus reached her and saw that the belt was free, but the man had a firm grip on the arm rest and wouldn't let go. Marcus and the stewardess, and now the woman beside the man who called him by his first name, Henry, convinced Marcus she was his wife, finally convinced her husband to let go and that Marcus would catch him. Marcus was in position to keep him from falling and asked him to put his foot out so that he could support it with his hand. Samantha asked for his hand. Marcus was in the correct position to catch the man, but not his wife, who fell when he did. The two dropped onto Marcus knocking both him and the stewardess down. All four of them were against the window or the overhead storage compartment in what was Marcus' row. The woman was the first to get up. She helped Henry and the two started toward the front of the plane. It was easier to walk on the overhead compartment than the arm rests. Samantha managed to get up and put out a hand to help Marcus. Marcus started toward the opening when Samantha said that she would follow him.

He proceeded to the opening and when he turned back to see if Samantha was following, he saw her with what looked like all the plane's blankets that she could carry. Once he was out of the plane he could see that several passengers were bloody and saw blood on the snow. Passengers were hurt either in a fall or were cut by the wreckage. He also noticed that some had vomit on their shirts or blouses. At least two men had pissed their pants. He didn't know if anyone did worse. He guessed about a hundred yards or more away he could see the burning front of the plane. He told all to get away from the plane.

Leaving the group of passengers, he began to walk to the burning wreckage and find if anyone there had survived. He had gone only a few steps when five other men joined him. On the way, he could see seats.

There were two pairs, in some way bolted together, all torn free of the plane. Each seat had a dead passenger still fastened to them. He could not see any major injury from the crash. He just accepted that they were dead. He continued to look and saw two sets of three seats. One set rested on its back. Marcus could see that it still had passengers strapped in it and they were alive. Marcus immediately went to it and with help from a man accompanying him, they were able to tip it up and found two passengers, a man and a woman in the first set of three seats still alive. The third seat was empty. They for some reason didn't unfasten their seat belts, they just sat there in a daze. The cold and snow were unable to jar them out of their stupor. He bent down, asked if they were hurt and saw the woman shake her head no. He thought he heard a no from the man. He freed them and pulled both to their feet. Both seemed groggy and needed to be supported. Two of the men with Marcus steadied them said they would return them to their original group at the tail of the plane. A third passenger in the second set of three seats was also alive, the two other seats were empty. The man was struggling with the seat belt clasp. Marcus helped the passenger release the seat belt and helped him to stand and he seemed as disoriented as the first two. He would also need help returning to the group at the tail of the plane. Another of the men who accompanied Marcus helped steady him and began to walk this third passenger back to the tail group. A miracle these three weren't killed or seriously injured. He wondered why the seats were unoccupied. Could the dead passengers they found have come from these seats? As Marcus and the remaining two men with him continued to look for additional seats, spotted five single seats each with a dead passenger. They left the dead people where they were. He and two men with him spotted three single unoccupied seats. Five more bodies could be seen and were being covered with snow and when Marcus checked, all were dead. He said to look around for more, but none were found but several pieces of luggage were spotted. He didn't know if the suitcases came from the front or the rear of the plane when it spun around. Marcus and the others approached the burning wreckage but because of the heat could not get close enough to see if any others had made it. When the wind shifted and blew toward them from the plane, he could smell burning fuel, and the plastic of the plane mixed with burning flesh. He had seen dead bodies during his career and the smell of decomposing flesh, but none compared with this smell. He was sure he would never forget it.

The snow and wind were getting worse and when they turned to return, they could just barely see their group. The wind picked up the snow causing a white out. Marcus said to the others to gather up all the luggage they could find and take it back to the others. He made one final check of the area for more bodies, didn't see any, grabbed two suitcases and joined the others returning to their group.

Marcus' rescue party reached the tail group and he could see people standing in a bunch twenty yards away from the tail section and they were shivering. He reported to what they had seen, there were no other survivors. The two he saw from the rear of the plane that were bloody were lying in the snow but wrapped in the plane's blankets. A woman was tending to the man with the bloody head wound, she had a cloth and wrapped it around his head. Several had bloody faces that he believed occurred when they dropped from their seats. None were serious he heard the woman who was wrapping the head of the hurt man. He was soon to learn that she was nurse Wells. The second wrapped in a blanket on the snow, was a woman. She had her neck wrapped with a bloody shirt. Marcus was unable to see but would learn later she had a bad cut on her right arm and a slash on her right side of her neck. The woman with the broken arm had a make-shift splint of a magazine wrapped around the break and tied with what looked like a torn-up shirt. A man and a woman were kneeling in the snow. He had his arm around her shoulder, and they were praying. Several others had the plane's blankets wrapped around them. Three were in shock, two were the ones rescued from the seats torn from the plane and walked in a circle around the group in a dazed fashion. Marcus had not paid much attention to the fact but knew for the most part, the group of passengers were not dressed for this type of weather. They left a warm east coast and were headed to a pleasant San

Francisco climate. Several were wearing sandals, shorts, and short sleeve shirts or T's. He was not overly dressed but wore jeans, a long sleeve shirt, a jacket and lace up shoes. He didn't remember when, but at some time on the flight, he had put on his sport coat. Marcus opened one of the suitcases and began to hand out items of clothing. He instructed those with sandals to find socks, dirty or clean, and to put them on. Anything that would fit should be used by others. Those with soiled clothes he said should be discarded before it froze on the passengers.

Marcus returned to the plane, entered, and opened the undamaged overhead compartment on the right side of the plane. He gathered as much of the clothing as he could and struggled toward the opening. Again, he began passing out the clothing. He saw the nurse scramble for a suitcase of clothes and grabbed several bras. Marcus believed the suitcase was most likely hers until he saw her make a sling out of them for the woman with the broken arm. Passengers were on their cell phones and he heard cursing when they could not get a reception. He heard someone ask how there could be a blizzard in the beginning of October. Another asked where they were. He heard an answer, "An early weather phenomena, a freak early blizzard and we are somewhere in the mountains of Colorado." A quick response to the question, a man wanted to know if the answerer was a meteorologist. Marcus heard him say, "No, but the current conditions tell me it's so." There was more bickering when someone asked if they should get away from the plane's tail. What if it should catch fire? Samantha answered that fuel was in the wings.

A young woman in the group asked the first intelligent question, "Why then did we come out of the plane into this hostile weather? And it's getting worse." No one had a good answer to that. It appeared to Marcus that everyone had the same idea that he had, get out of the plane. The next question from the shivering young woman was directed to Samantha, "How long will it be before we are rescued?"

Everyone looked at her for an answer, "They know we went down and approximately where. First, we must be located and then a rescue team will be sent. With the weather as bad as it is, if the wreckage is not covered by snow, I'd say two, three, maybe more days."

Marcus said to Samantha so that most of the group could hear, "Maybe we should go back inside of the plane, get out of the wind and snow?"

Someone asked, "How will we get back over the seats? If we stay on the one side of the plane it will become very crowded."

Marcus had an answer to that, "That's logical. But when I returned from the burning front of the plane, beneath the seating area I saw the cargo hold. It has curved walls and a few pieces of bracing but all we will need to do is step into it." There was a general agreement among the survivors that it was a good idea. There was a floor, space, in what would be the belly of the plane and when the plane was torn open wires and tubing could now be seen. He never asked but assumed that luggage would have been stacked in this area but had been thrown out when the tail spun around. He helped Samantha get everyone in and as far back as a bulkhead would allow. He got three men to help him lift the blanket the head wounded man was on and carried him into the plane. Nurse Wells helped the hurt woman get up and that is when Marcus saw her right arm wrapped. Marcus learned that the two had been at the break of the fuselage. Samantha helped the woman with the broken arm.

It was cold in the cargo hold but a lot less wind and snow. Someone suggested a fire. Marcus exited the plane with another man and proceeded to the nearest pine trees. Both looked for dead wood. The two returned to the plane with an armful of wood. A torn magazine provided the initial fire to start the wood burning. The small fire may have heated the interior belly of the plane, but the cold passengers never found out. The one thing they did become aware of was that the fire they started soon filled the space with smoke. Passenger began choking and coughing. The wind outside the plane kept the smoke from exiting. The fire was a good idea but was not going to work. The passengers could and would withstand the cold but not the smoke.

Could Marcus some way keep the wind and snow out? He asked if anyone had safety pins on them. Somehow, they came up with a dozen. He grabbed two blankets from passengers and told Samantha to pin the two blankets together and then get one more. As best as he could guess, Marcus believed the opening was as much as eight feet or more in height. With help from two of the men, he attached the blankets as high as they could reach to the torn metal of the opening to keep out some of the wind and snow. The blankets did keep much of the wind and snow out and light so that the belly of the tail section became dim. "Everyone huddle together for warmth as best as you can. Hug each other," he said to the group. "Make good use of the blankets not used by the injured. Any extra clothing should be on top of you." Without being asked he took charge and was looked upon as their leader and his words were heeded. He whispered to Samantha, "How many made it?"

She whispered back to him, "As best I could count, forty-seven, including the two who are hurt. I don't remember seeing your friend, the scotch drinker."

"He was not my friend, just met him this morning," Marcus replied. "Everyone is settled as best they can be, are there any more blankets and is there any food?"

"No blankets. All I had in the rear is a dozen or so packs of peanuts and some bottled water. Food would have been in the forward galley and it's gone," she replied.

The belly of the plane that they were now in had a wall with a door centered in it, but now was horizontal and maybe three or four feet from the side of the cargo hold, or their now floor. He could see that it was slightly ajar and suggested that maybe it would be better on the other side. It would be difficult getting the passengers up to it and it would be dark on the other side. He wanted to know if there might be anything they could use on the other side. Samantha believed there wouldn't be and believed the airplane's electronic equipment was there. "I'll sit and rest for a few minutes and go back inside the plane for the peanuts and any carry-on cases I can find. Maybe later check behind the bulkhead."

He was close enough to Samantha to see her shivering and shaking. He said, "Come here. You are cold and shivering," and he removed his sport coat and put it around her. He took her in his arms and hugged her. They leaned back against the curved side. He began to vigorously rub her back. After a moment, he said, "Salvaging from the plane can wait."

She whispered into his ear, "If we are going to this intimate, I think you can start calling me Sam." He stopped rubbing her back and repeated the procedure on her arms. After five minutes, he returned to her back. He could feel her shivering less. She again whispered and asked, "How will we be able to survive maybe four days or more?"

Marcus could hear the concern and worry in her voice. He answered, "Don't think about it. Let's just get by one day at a time." She wasn't the only one concerned. He could hear crying and was sure the woman he saw praying outside was praying again.

Nurse Wells crawled to them and said, "Maybe the two of you should get a room. Getting serious, I believe the man with the head wound has a concussion and has slipped into a coma. He needs hospitalization. The guy you found from the front of the plane is still dazed and acting irrational."

"There's nothing more we can do for the guy in the coma," Marcus said. "Keep him warm and comfortable as possible. Have a person lie down on both sides of him. If no one will volunteer to do it, come and get me and I will. The irrational guy, I don't know except talking to him and get through to him. Maybe he will be able to grasp the seriousness of our situation."

Samantha said, "We will talk to him if you think it will do any good and I'll lie on the other side of the guy in the coma."

"I don't think you will do any better than I have, but thanks," nurse Wells said.

Blowing wind could easily be heard as the group became quiet and the crying subsided but could still be heard. Several whispered the same words that Samantha had, "What are we going to do?" They would just have to bear it. It was mid-afternoon and Marcus didn't want to let go of

Sam. She was warm and felt good, but he knew he must if he was going to go top side before it got dark. He believed that she had fallen asleep, so he didn't move but just held her.

Marcus heard a noise to his right and looked and saw a woman crawling to him. When she was within touching distance, she tapped him on the leg and whispered, "Are you awake?"

"Yes," he replied.

Sam stirred in his arms and asked "Yes what? Who is it?"

"My name's Gail,' she said. "What was that noise?"

Marcus replied, "It's just the wind blowing across the plane's torn metal."

"No." she said. "Listen."

Sam was awake now and told him, "I heard it too. Sounds like an animal."

The woman asked, "Could it be wolves? How about a bear or a mountain lion?"

Marcus listened, he tried to shut out the wind and he heard it also. "It sounds like a donkey braying, but that's impossible."

Then to their astonishment they heard a man call out, "Is there anyone in there?" Marcus heard the question repeated, "Hello! Anyone in there?"

Chapter 2

Marcus rose and went to the makeshift blanket door and looked out. Standing near the seating area of the tail section he saw a man and a mule. "Here!" he shouted. "We are here!" Other passengers heard Marcus and excitement quickly spread through the group and several began to rise. Beyond belief Marcus was talking to someone, a rescuer. No one gave any thought to the fact that it was too soon for them to have been found. The man led the mule to the cargo hold opening and tied it to a jagged piece of metal and he stepped into the cargo hold followed by a gust of wind and snow. Marcus saw a man of an indeterminate age dressed for the weather in what Marcus thought were dirty work clothes, gloves, and in desperate need of a shave and a haircut. His hat was tied down with a scarf that went over his ears. Marcus asked him who he was and could he help them.

He removed his glove and stuck out his hand to Marcus and said, "Name's Ellery. Heard the explosion and though I saw smoke through the snow, came to see what happened."

Marcus introduced himself and behind him a passenger asked if he could help them, call for help. Ellery answered the question with a no. He couldn't call, no telephone. Marcus was the next to ask, "What can you do for us? How close are we to help, a town?"

Before he could answer Samantha asked, "Is there anyone else nearby that can help?"

"No," replied Ellery. "Nearest town is Twin Pines, 'bout fifteen miles from here. All I can do is point the way and offer you my cabin, 'bout a mile and a half, two miles from here." He surveyed the group and continued, "I think you all would fit. Will be warmer, you're welcome to it but it's going to be a hoof. If you want I can lead ya'."

"We have some people who are hurt, one guy is serious and will not be able to walk," nurse Wells said. "Others we can assist."

Ellery was quiet for a moment, then he said, "You can throw him across my mule, Bailey."

She didn't respond to Ellery's suggestion. Marcus saw a look of concern on the nurse's face and he knew she did not think that was a very viable proposal, so he spoke up, "Maybe four of us men can carry him by his blanket."

"How 'bout you wrap him up good in a couple of blankets, I'll put a rope around his chest and under his shoulders and I'll let Bailey pull him over the snow?"

Marcus remembered how difficult it was carrying the hurt man in the blanket just to get him into the cargo hold. It was not the best idea but under the circumstances was probably the best solution. "Okay he said," Before the nurse could say anything, he added, "Only other option is that you stay here with him until a rescue party arrives." Without waiting for a response, Marcus began to take down the make-shift blanket covering, unpinned it, and he, Sam and the nurse wrapped the hurt man as best that they could in three of the blankets and took a piece of rope from Ellery and wrapped it around him to keep the blankets in place. Ellery tied a rope over his chest and under the man's shoulders and attached it to his mule.

Ellery took a length of rope from a funny looking saddle on the mule, tied one end to the saddle and said that they should all should grab hold of it, use it for support and so that no one would wonder away from the group because of the storm. Nurse Wells said she would walk along side of the blanket wrapped man the mule would be pulling and try and keep his head up so he would not hit anything in the snow. Sam said she would help the woman with the broken arm and two men volunteered to support and help the woman who was cut. Marcus would bring up the rear and make sure no one wandered away. Everyone was encouraged to wrap their feet in any extra clothing that they had. After ten minutes they were ready.

Ellery started and they all followed behind him. Marcus could see that the storm had gotten worse. He wasn't sure if it was still snowing hard or that the wind was blowing around what had already fallen. When he looked toward the smoldering front of the plane he could barely make it out and several times it was completely whited out. The tracks he and the other made walking to it were completely obliterated. On occasion the wind picked up the snow and blew across the caravan so hard that he could not see Ellery. The going was rough for the group, they had trouble trying to stay caught up because of the snow even though it was only about four or five inches deep. Marcus saw several fall and be assisted by their traveling companions to get back on their feet and helped along. It had not been planned but he had to circle around and go to Ellery and told him they would have to stop and rest four times during the two-mile trek. What would have been maybe a half hour walk without the snow and stragglers, turned into over two and a half hours. Several passengers didn't want to stop, the sooner they got to his cabin the better. But others were so tired that if they didn't stop and rest, they were not going to make it.

When they finally reached Ellery's cabin it was beginning to get dark. Most of the passengers were having a difficult time walking in the snow which was almost six inches deep near the cabin. Marcus could see the cabin was up against a rocky hill and he could see what looked like two out-buildings. Ellery tied the mule to a porch post, pulled open the door and went inside. The others followed and they saw him throw an armful of wood on the smoldering fire in the fireplace. He went back outside before he was asked any questions and they saw him untie the man his mule had dragged and then lead his mule away. The group of passengers shook off the snow clinging to them and crowded around the fire as close as possible. Marcus got several men to help him and the nurse carry the hurt man into the cabin and made his way through the crowd to get the man near the heat. It was not overly warm in the cabin but compared to the cold of the plane it seemed like heaven.

When Marcus entered, he looked around and saw that it was a two-room cabin. The inside had been finished off but needed paint. The room that they were in served as a kitchen and most likely the dining area. There were shelves and an empty cupboard missing its door. Both were near empty except for some spices and several almost empty sacks. Pots and pans and dishes with several forks, spoons and a knife were sitting on a shelf above a wood burning cook stove. There was a table with two chairs, one broken. It had a sink but no running water. He saw several partially burned candles and two kerosene hurricane lanterns. On both sides of the fireplace the walls were stacked with wood of various thicknesses, from the floor to almost the ceiling. Near the cook stove was a box with smaller pieces of wood and kindling. Exploring the other room Marcus found it was the bedroom with several double bunk beds and a four-drawer dresser. Only one bunk had blankets and sheets. On a wall were hooks with clothes and what Marcus believed to be two head lamps. There were several work shoes and boots. Near the boots, he saw a blue can that he believed to be bigger than a gallon but not as big as a five-gallon bucket. On its side he read, CARBIDE. If his memory served him correctly it was used as a gas supply for the head lamps. All in all, the cabin interior was very Spartan.

Ellery came from outside through a door in the bedroom. In the kitchen, he lit the two lanterns and hung one from a post and one on the table. He let everyone know that the toilet was out back and to the right and he had tied a rope from the cabin to it so no one would wander off and get lost. One of the out-buildings Marcus had seen was not a building but only a roof that served as the mule's shelter. The passengers knew he said he had no food and said he had only enough for him to last a week before he packed up Bailey and would head out for Twin Pines. The one thing he had a lot of was tea and they were welcome to it, but he had no sugar. Water was in a bucket by the sink, use it all and he would go to his spring and get more. It had a pipe coming from a mountain spring behind his cabin and water ran through it. It was close to thirty yards from the outhouse. Without being asked he went to the sink and poured water into a kettle and hung it in the fireplace. "You'll have to share one of my two tin cups," he told the group.

In the dim light of the cabin Marcus saw what he thought was a real character, someone from a movie. He asked, "You live here?"

"No. Me and Bailey head out the middle of October." He verified the comment of one of the passengers when he said, "Never seen a blizzard this early, probably will melt soon. Sure do hope so. Don't want to try and make it to Twin Pines with snow on the ground."

"If you don't live here, why are you here and what do you do?" Samantha asked.

"I'm a squatter and I got a mine out back, I'm also prospector, I dig for gold," he replied.

Marcus asked, "Do you ever find any?"

"Just enough to get by. But someday, I'm gonna hit it big," Ellery replied.

Marcus said under his breath to Sam, "The dream of every prospector."

"So, who does this cabin belong to?" Samantha asked.

"Belongs to a bunch of rich elk hunters who built it. Didn't know that spring melt and rain washed out a couple of hundred yards of the road every spring. Plus, the elk hunting in these parts wasn't good, so they sort of abandoned it and 'bout five year ago. I took it over."

"What are the chances that we can walk out to Twin Pines?" the young woman who asked why leave the plane, asked.

He looked at the group, most of them so tired out walking from the plane that they were nodding off, "Not good. I wouldn't try it. Not in this weather, 'specially the women. If it breaks, follow the outline of the road." At this statement, Marcus and several passengers looked at one of the windows in the kitchen and they could see from the small amount of light from the lanterns, snow flying by it and could hear the wind blowing.

By this time most of the passengers had staked out a spot near the fireplace. Many took off their outer layers of clothes and put them as close as possible to the fireplace to dry. Many huddled together for warmth. Ellery made two big cups of tea, but many of the group were too spent to try any. He took all the soiled bedding off his bunk and passed it out for the passengers to share. He sat against the wall close to Marcus and Samantha.

Marcus was near Sam to the side of the fireplace. They were sitting against a wood stack, his arm around her shoulder. He said he would try to keep awake and keep the fire burning. She should try and get some sleep. She snuggled close to him and whispered into his ear, "I want to thank you for all that you did getting passengers out of the plane and to here."

He whispered back, "If I hadn't done it, someone else would have."

"No," she said. "We couldn't have done it without your help. You stepped up and took charge and the passengers listened to you."

"When we get out of here you can thank me with dinner."

"It's a date," she replied.

In no time, it appeared that almost everyone was asleep, regardless of the conditions and that they were on a hard floor. Marcus did not stay awake to feed the fire. He tried, but after an hour, he also fell asleep. He had just nodded off when Gail, the woman who told him on the plane that she heard something, was shaking his leg and whispered, "Wake up!"

"What's wrong?" he whispered.

"It's me, Gail. There's someone at the door," she answered.

"It's just the wind, no one could be out there," Marcus said to her.

"No, listen," was her response.

Their whispering wakened Samantha and she asked, "What is it?"

"She believes she heard someone at the door," he told her.

All three listened, they heard nothing. After a moment, Gail said, "You're probably right. How could anyone be out there?"

"Let me up Sam, I'm going to throw a couple of pieces of wood on the fire," Marcus told his companion.

"Wait Marcus! I heard it too. There is someone out there!" she said in a whisper. "Maybe someone we overlooked, from the front of the plane."

"Okay, I'll check," said Marcus. He freed himself from Sam, threw two pieces of wood on the fire and walked between passengers asleep on the floor. He reached the door and opened it. He was surprised when Agent Beale fell into the room. He was able to catch him before he hit the floor and before the wind blew the door closed on him. Half lifting and half dragging, Marcus was able to drag the cold and wet agent near to the fireplace. The movement of Marcus and Samantha wakened Ellery and several passengers. "Sam help me get him near the fire." They put the agent down. "His clothes are frozen and so is he. Ellery, throw a few more pieces of wood on the fire. Sam wake the nurse."

Marcus was rubbing Beale's hands when the nurse reached them. She looked at him and felt him. "Get him out of those wet clothes and his shoes off, wrap a blanket around him," she said. Marcus helped her undress Beale.

Samantha asked, "How is he?"

Nurse Wells said, "He's almost frozen. He is awfully cold, maybe fingertips have frost bite. Ellery, make some hot tea. Keep rubbing his hands. I'll do a foot." Addressing Gail, the young woman who woke Marcus up, the nurse said to her, "You rub the other one. It's almost midnight, went down around eleven on my watch. He's been out there in the cold for about twelve hours."

Marcus could see his lips moving and heard Beale mumbling. He told the agent to be quiet, they could talk tomorrow. Ellery brought a tin cup of hot tea to him. Marcus said, "It ain't scotch but it'll have to do." Except for Sam, Marcus knew none of the others would know what he was talking about. The nurse lifted his head and Ellery held the cup to his lips and tilted it. Beale drank some of the hot liquid and Marcus could hear him give out a satisfied, "Ahh."

It appeared to the people around him that after about ten minutes Beale was making a quick and good recovery even though he was still shivering. Marcus asked him, "Where did you go?"

Marcus could see him smile and he heard just above a whisper, "I, I, I took, took some. A suitcase full. Thought I could find my way out of here. Got lost. Lost my gun."

Nurse Wells asked, "What is he talking about."

Marcus uttered, "He said he was escorting something valuable in the cargo hold."

Gail who had been quiet to this point asked, "What?"

Marcus answered her, "He didn't say." His next question was directed to Beale, "How did you find us?"

Beale again whispering said, "Smelled smoke, saw your light. Walked and crawled till I got here."

"Here, take another drink of this," Ellery said.

Beale sipped some of the hot tea, waited a moment and said, "Money, a suitcase full of money. I took it," he was able to get out.

Curious, Samantha asked, "Where is it?"

Beale smiled and said, "Hid it. There's millions more, millions."

"Be quiet now, everyone back to sleep. We will deal with it tomorrow." He put a blanket over Agent Beale, and everyone went back to their previous positions. Soon Marcus and Sam were also asleep.

The next morning sun could be seen as it came through the window. It had stopped snowing and the wind had died down. It appeared it was going to be a nice day. The fire was burning. Passengers were beginning to stir; Marcus was one of them. He stretched and looked around at all the passengers. To no one in particular he asked where Ellery was. A man near the bedroom door said that a half hour ago, he threw wood on the fire and said time was a-wasting, he was going to his mine out back. Sam stirred against Marcus' chest and he whispered, "It has cleared up, help should be here soon. I'm going to let everyone sleep," he said to her.

"How's Beale?" she asked.

"He looks like he's asleep. Let me up, I'm going to check on the injured passengers," and Marcus rose.

The man who said Ellery went to his mine was standing and looking into the bedroom. Marcus walked to each of the three passengers who were hurt, none showed any sign that they were awake. The man who told him where Ellery was said, "I can see his mine through the bedroom window and there's his mule. Funny though, smoke is coming from the mine opening."

Marcus walked over to where the passenger was standing and looked out through the window. "What's your name," he asked. He heard the man answer Phil Dobson. As soon as he saw what Phil described as smoke coming from Ellery's mine, Marcus said, "That's not smoke! It's dust!" He ran through the bedroom, opened the door and ran to the mine. Phil followed him. The two entered the mine. Light from outside showed that the mine had caved in about twenty yards from the opening. From what Marcus could see, much more of the mine had caved and passage deeper into the mine would be impossible. Ellery had been caught inside the mine and there was no way to get to him. Marcus cautiously approached the cave-in and when he got close to it, he saw Ellery. A large timber had fallen on him and crushed him. Marcus felt for a pulse, there wasn't one. The two men carefully tried to lift the timber, but it had rock debris on the other end and was difficult. Marcus picked up a smaller broken piece of a log and used it as a lever to lift. When he did more of the roof of the mine fell. "Quick! Pull him out Phil!" he shouted. When Ellery was free the two men half lifted, half carried and dragged the man to the mine's entrance. Once outside of the mine they laid him down on a snow drift close to the cabin. Marcus checked for a pulse and didn't find one. "He's dead. I'd like to cover him, but can't spare a blanket," Marcus said. "Let's get back inside."

Once inside he told all the people awake that Ellery was dead, his mine caved in on him. Someone said they needed to look over what food he did have and make good use of it. Someone else suggested they look for what gold Ellery may have found. Several women began to rummage around on his kitchen shelves and looked in the small cupboard. He saw them pull out several almost empty sacks. One started a fire in the cook stove. The other sent a man out to fetch more water from the spring's pipe that Eller had mentioned. After two hours, the women had cooked beans and baked some bread. The men who looked for any gold Ellery may have found, came up empty.

While all of this was happening, nurse Wells sidled over to where Marcus and Samantha were standing. "Can I speak to you?" she asked him. He told her yes and wanted to know what about. "He is dead," she said.

"That is what I told everyone," Marcus said.

"No. Not Ellery." Marcus was prepared to hear her say the man with the head injury he thought was sleeping had died, but she surprised him when she continued, "The agent, Beale," she said. "I know he could be suffering hypothermia, but I thought he would live. Didn't seem that bad off."

Marcus didn't say anything, he just shrugged his shoulder as if to say things happen. He got Phil, the guy that went to the mine with him, the two forced their way through the group of passengers and carried the dead agent outside and put him with Ellery. "No sense leaving him here inside where everyone could see him." It took only seconds before everyone knew, but they were focused on the food that the two women had prepared and their survival. Like the passengers in the front of the plane, they didn't know either man, nor were they interested in the two bodies outside.

It was after noon and all the food that could be found had been eaten. Like Ellery said, the snow wouldn't last. Water could be seen through the windows dripping off the roof as the snow melted. People had been using the outdoor toilet most of the morning and when Marcus needed to go, he noticed quite a change in the weather. It was beginning to get warm. When he came back inside the cabin he told Samantha if they weren't found, he would attempt to walk to Twin Pines and get help. The passengers were not comfortable, but the situation was a lot better than it was yesterday and they were alive.

It seemed clear to everyone they would just have to wait to be rescued. Marcus kept the fire burning and people huddled together and wrapped blankets or clothes around themselves. It was mid-afternoon when Gail walked to where Marcus was sitting with Samantha against the wall. She touched his leg with her foot to get his attention. When he looked up at her she asked, "What is that noise?" Like before, Marcus said he couldn't hear anything.

Sam had heard her, and she said in an excited voice, "It's a helicopter!"

Others heard her and some ran to the door and were outside and waving their arms. Marcus could hear the passengers outside cheering. Sam got up and walked to the door and said to those outside, "They won't be able to be hear or see you but they will eventually find us." None of the people outside paid any attention to her.

Chapter 3

Three days later Marcus was sitting at a conference room table in the two-story Twin Pines Motel. On the table was a small box of coffee and a stack of paper cups with sugar packets and non-dairy creams. Off to one side was a doughnut box. He would not be the only one questioned by the two standing in front of him. He refused a doughnut and could see through the window that there was still snow on the ground where it had drifted, but most of it had melted. Quite a bit of slush in the parking lot and on the edges of the sidewalks. He believed that there would be more questions about the plane crash. He told all that he knew yesterday to investigators. It wasn't much, but he assumed that by retelling it, maybe he would include something that he may have overlooked the first time. What more could he add? The engines failed and the plane crashed and broke apart. He was in a section of the plane that people lived. That's all he knew or could tell. The investigators yesterday were not interested in how the passengers survived by going to a prospector's cabin, nor did they show an interest in the fact that another passenger, Treasury Agent Beale had died. No one asked about the dead prospector. He was not their concern. The investigators wanted to know what he could tell them about the plane's engines failing, what may have led up to the plane's problems. One caught fire while he was asleep, the other exploded, that was it. He could add nothing more.

Standing across the table from him was a smartly dressed woman with short, cropped hair, wore glasses, probably in her late forties. She appeared serious and most likely would lead the conversation. Beside her was a young man Marcus guessed about thirty, and like the woman, well dressed in a suit and tie. In front of him was a portable tape recorder, both had note pads and a coffee cup. Yesterday one of the investigators only took notes and had not provided coffee.

"I'm special Treasury Agent Cory Larson and my partner here," and she pointed to the younger man, "is Agent Jeffrey Turner. He will be recording everything said here. Will you have a problem with that?" She stuck out her hand and Marcus rose and shook it. At the same time, he shook his head and mumbled, "No." He turned and shook the hand of Agent Turner. Introductions made, the three sat.

As soon as they were seated, the detective had to ask why they were not armed. Cory Larson answered, "Treasury agents don't carry a weapon unless they were going to go into a potentially dangerous situation. This is not a situation that warrant us carrying weapons."

Detective Rothman was satisfied with the answer and after a moment Agent Turner asked, "You are Detective Marcus Rothman from San Francisco?"

He nodded his head yes. He knew that they were being recorded and said for them to hear, "Yes." He took a drink of his coffee and shook his head no when the woman pointed to the box of doughnuts.

Ms. Larson said, "We are not connected to the airline investigation force. We need to ask you a few questions, but not about the crash."

Marcus was curious and asked, "What then?"

Ms. Larson simply asked, "What happened to the money that was on the plane Mr. Rothman? That is what we want to know."

The detective was a little taken aback and quickly reasoned that sooner or later someone would have to be concerned about the money that Agent Beale had talked about and the suitcase of money that was missing. "All I know is what Agent Beale told me. He said he took a suitcase of it and hid it. That's all I know, and you can call me Marcus."

"When we checked the plane none of it was there. There was a lot, fifteen aluminum metal cases and they couldn't have just walked away. If

Agent Beale took one, we want to know what happened to the remaining fourteen?" Agent Turner said.

Marcus thought about what he just heard and answered, "How much money are you talking about?" Neither of the treasury people said anything. So, Marcus continued, "Maybe it was in the front and was burned up."

"No," said Ms. Larson. "It was loaded in the rear behind the last bulkhead and a preliminary inspection of the wreckage showed no evidence of even a partial case."

"Well," Marcus said, "when the tail spun around, they must have been thrown out. We did find several passenger suitcases that were thrown out of the plane's spinning tail. Most likely that was what happened."

"Did you see any metal cases among the passenger suit cases Detective Rothman?" Agent Turner asked.

Marcus had to say, "No. Call me Marcus, please."

"Besides, the cases were behind a cargo net and it was still there and intact," Agent Turner continued.

The next question came from Ms. Larson. "Did anyone leave the cabin during the night?"

"Everyone was dead on their feet, tired from walking in the snow and we were all cold," replied Marcus. "No one left. No one was dressed to be outside in the blizzard. If someone did leave I wouldn't have known. I fell asleep shortly after we got to the cabin, had to be awakened when Beale showed up. If someone did leave, in that weather, with the wind blowing and the snow, no one would have even known the direction of the plane, let alone in the dark. Couldn't have followed our tracks from the plane because the snow covered everything almost as soon as we walked."

"Could Agent Beale have taken it all?" asked Agent Turner.

"I don't know. When he came to the cabin he was in really bad shape. Almost frozen and the nurse said his fingers may have frost bite. He definitely said he took a suitcase full of it. But fifteen cases, I don't know." he paused and again asked for the second time, "how much is a lot?"

"Who all knew about the money, heard what Beale said?" Agent Turner asked.

Marcus answered, "Me for sure, Ms. Wells, Samantha, the miner Ellery, and Gail, a passenger who heard him at the cabin door. Maybe a few other passengers who were near us. I really don't know."

Ms. Larson looked at her notes and said, "That would be nurse Wells, flight attendant Samantha Wright, the dead miner and Gail Mackey. Doubt they could have become a gang. Could it have been someone else on the plane? Maybe from the front? Someone thrown free, not killed. There were several empty seats scattered around. How many bodies did you see?"

Marcus thought back to the burning plane and counted in his mind what he remembered and said, "If my memory serves me right, there were ten or eleven."

"Possible you missed anybody?" Agent Turner asked.

"Don't think so," replied Marcus. "I checked everyone I could find. They were either dead or the seats were empty. How would anyone in the front of the plane even know about the money? Agent Beale did tell me his partner was in the front. He would have known about it. Maybe he didn't die and was thrown free."

Ms. Larson said, "It is going to take several weeks to identify all of the bodies and find out if anyone is missing."

"No one on the plane could have done this. Anyone first on the scene see any tracks going from the plane to here? See tracks going anywhere?" Marcus asked.

"As far as we know, no, but the blowing snow could have covered them. Don't even know which direction Beale might have come from," she replied. "Do you have any idea the direction he walked?"

"No. Opened the door and he fell into my arms and I pulled him into the cabin and closed the door. Never looked outside," was all that Marcus could say. They were all quiet for a moment when Marcus asked, "You never did answer my question about the money, how much was a lot?"

Ms. Larson looked directly at him and said, "One hundred and sixteen million."

"Wow!" responded Marcus. "To take that much would have taken more than one person, or one person making several trips. Maybe it was Agent Beale. Nurse Wells estimated he was outside for about twelve hours. When I helped the nurse undress him, I noticed he was in good physical shape. I guess it could be possible Beale took it all." There was a lull in the conversation before Marcus said, "You know, no one ever saw any money. Are you sure it was on the plane?"

Ms. Larson replied, "It was, and Agent Beale told you he took some, didn't he?"

"Yes, he did say that," Marcus replied. "But whether he saw it or not I don't know."

"It's warming enough to melt the snow, so we will begin our search for it. We will be able to find what Beale said he hid and the rest of it," Agent Turner said with a note of surety in the way he said it.

Chapter 4

It was the first week in March, over two years since the airplane incident and Marcus was driving to his apartment. Sam was with him. They were making small talk about the dinner they just had and if they would ever go back to the restaurant. Marcus said, "It was a place that Regis suggested. Said it was pretty good. Glad you met me after work, didn't have to go home and change and then drive to the restaurant."

Her response was, "I wouldn't pay much attention to what your partner tells you in the future. I don't know if the food was good or not, there was so much time between the courses. I got filled up on the bread."

"Maybe that was their plan. The service may have been slow but I liked my chicken," he said. "We could ask next time to be served everything at the same time Sam. The scallop you gave me was good."

"I'll think about it, but right now it is not a restaurant high on my list of places to go eat," she replied. "I'm off tomorrow, what do you say we just sleep in, get up and go and have pancakes?"

"Sounds like a good idea to me," Marcus replied.

"Marcus, could we stop at Kelly's on the way home. I'd like to get something for my throat," she said.

"You coming down with something?" he asked.

"Don't know. Hope not. My throat feels a bit rough, I might be," she said. "These late winter sore throats can be a real pain."

Marcus pulled into the parking lot at the side of the convenience store and got out with Sam and the two went into the store. When they entered the store, Marcus saw six other customers. He paid them no mind and headed to the ice cream freezer and picked out a half gallon of butter pecan. Then went to the cookie section and picked up a bag of chocolate chip cookies. Sam was talking to the owner Kelly Shang. He could hear her ask him how his daughter was doing and could see him holding a small paper bag open. To her side was a small pile of items she had picked out.

"Okay I guess. The wife says not to worry, women been having babies for thousands of years," Marcus heard Kelly say. Then he heard Sam reply, "I'm sure she will be alright. Tell her I said hello."

Sam moved aside when one of the customers came to the checkout counter where she and Kelly had been talking. The customer put several items on the counter and Kelly began to ring them up. When he asked if that will be all the customer's companion yelled to him not to forget a pack of Camels. Kelly reached behind him, opened a cabinet with glass doors, got the cigarettes and put them in the bag with the other items. A third customer came to the counter and laid a bag of chips on it and said, "And these chips." The customer who yelled for the cigarettes said not to forget a pack of matches. Kelly rang up everything and told the first customer the total was twenty-three even. He paid, Kelly thanked him and said come back and all three left. They no sooner turned away from the counter when Sam and Kelly began to talk again as if they had not been interrupted.

"The baby will change their lives," Sam said.

"They are looking forward to it," Kelly said. "They were very grateful for the stroller you and Marcus gave them."

"What are you talking about?" Marcus asked as he put the ice cream and cookies on the counter.

Sam smiled and said, "Kelly's grandson to be." He rang up the items that Marcus had put on the counter as well as the items Sam had picked up and placed them in the bag.

"You will have to get a rocking chair so that you can rock him to sleep," Marcus continued.

"Already got one," replied Kelly. Done ringing up the items Sam and Marcus had purchased Kelly asked, "This all?"

When Marcus believed it was all they needed, he told Kelly yes and was told the total was twenty-two and twenty-three cents. Marcus paid him and he told them to have a good evening and the two left the store. They walked outside and around the corner of the store to their car and got in. They buckled up and Marcus began to back out when Sam said, "Damn!" and in a guilty pleading voice continued. "Don't get mad."

She was silent when Marcus spoke for her, "You didn't get anything for your throat, did you?"

"Just pull back into your spot and I'll run in and be right back," she replied.

Marcus pulled back into his spot and stopped. Sam put her purse over her shoulder, got out of the car and went around to the front of the store. Marcus left the motor running while he played with the radio dial. He did not find a station that he liked but settled on a song he was familiar with. The song was over and still Sam had not returned. He turned the car off and got out of the car and headed for the entrance. When he walked in he saw Sam behind the counter with Kelly, and in line, one of the customers he had seen in the store. "Sam, what is taking you so long?" he asked. "You and Kelly get started talking again? Let's go."

Sam faced him and at the same time she shouted, "Marcus! He's got a gun!"

At her words, Marcus moved to his side and drew his own weapon. Behind him the glass door exploded in a shower of glass when the bullet hit it. He was now to his right in the next aisle over when he yelled, "Get down Sam!" He didn't believe it would do any good, but he yelled to the shooter, "I'm a policeman. Put the gun down!"

The shooter reacted to Marcus' move by moving to the same aisle, gun ready, he fired again at Marcus as soon as he could see him and missed. Before the holdup man could shoot again Marcus shot and saw the man go down, his gun went flying. Staying where he was Marcus called out to Sam, "Sam are you alright?" He could see the counter but no Sam or Kelly. From behind the counter he heard her yell, "Marcus, there's two of them. We're okay."

"If you can reach the phone, dial 911 and ask for help. Tell the operator it's a 10-31, shots fired and give her the address. I'll get the other guy," he told her. Marcus moved left, back toward the other aisles and looked for the second holdup man. He heard a shot when a can of something on the shelf beside him burst open as the bullet hit it. Marcus was ready to move into the third aisle where he believed the shooter was, but instead of just popping into the aisle, he dropped to one knee as he entered the aisle. He heard as well as saw the second holdup man shoot over his head. Marcus fired two shots and the man pitched backward onto the ice cream cooler glass door and slid down onto the floor. Marcus went to him, kicked his gun away and heard, "Hel…Help me. I nee' ambulance."

"Just lie still," he said to the shot man. "One's on the way." He went in the direction that he kicked the holdup man's gun into the aisle he had just left. Standing there was a woman. "Lady move away from the gun, I'm a policeman. Let me see your hands! Go stand by the counter."

"I'm not with these two. Just came in to buy some cigarettes," she said to him. "Don't shoot me, please. Is he going to be okay? I'll get his gun for you," she replied.

"Don't do it lady! Go up by the counter!" he yelled at her. But she didn't pay attention to what he said.

He heard her say, "I'll help," as she reached for the gun and grabbed hold of it by the butt. As she began to bring the gun up, Marcus cold see she had her finger on the trigger. "Drop it!" he yelled. "Put your hands up!"

As she rose he heard, "You wouldn't shoot a wom…" and he fired just as he heard sirens.

It was two months later when Marcus and Sam where at his partner Regis' backyard cook out and pool party. There were about ten other detectives and their families. It was still a little chilly, but his partner Regis had opened his pool and had gotten it ready for swimming. Several adults and most of the kids were swimming. The adults not swimming were eating, drinking beer or sodas, and where talking. Renee Calenda, Regis' wife, was talking to Sam. Sam asked, "How do you like being married to a detective?"

Renee answered, "We have a good marriage Sam, but I do worry about him every time he leaves the house." She quit talking about her husband for a moment, Marcus' partner Regis, when she yelled, "Shirley! Quit splashing your sister! You don't I'll make you get out of the pool!"

When she turned back, Sam said to her, "But he's not on the street. A lot of his time is spent on investigating, doesn't come in contact with criminal all of the time."

"But you never know," she replied. "It can always happen. Look what happened to you and Roth at that convenience store couple of months ago. How were either of you to know that the woman was with the holdup guys?"

"Marcus just made the right decision when he shot her," Sam replied.

"But if he would have hesitated a second longer, it might have been the other way around. Roth would have been shot," Renee said.

"Maybe you're right, but all of life is a gamble. You could be hit by a car, drown," and she pointed to the pool, "or get shot," was Sam's reply.

Renee didn't respond to Sam's remark. They were silent for a moment before Renee asked, "What about you and Roth? Either of you made any long-range plans?"

"No," answered Sam. "We haven't discussed the future. Right now, we are happy to be together and enjoying each other's company. I think the world of him."

"Uh oh," Renee said.

"What is it Renee?" Sam asked.

"Melinda is a little tipsy," said Renee. "Chris is edging her toward the pool. I think he's going to push her in, clothes and all." The two women were silent as they watched the two adults. It appeared that Melinda was oblivious to what Chris was intent on doing. It looked to Sam that just when he was about to make his move, Melinda moved and at the same time reached out and pulled Chris toward her, and into the pool he went. She had been aware of her husband Chris and what he had intend to do. Chris was flailing around in the water while all those sitting around the pool were pointing and laughing. From across where Sam and Renee were talking, they saw two men reach for Chris and pull him out. Renee saw her husband walk to him and she could hear him say, "Let's get you in the house and out of those wet clothes. I'll lend you some of mine." To his crowd of partiers, they heard him shout, "Everyone, we will be right back, keep partying," as they disappeared into the house.

Marcus approached the two women and asked, "Okay, what are you two conspiring about."

Renee looked up at him and answered, "Nothing special. You know women stuff, love, marriage, family vacations and such."

Marcus looked at her and said, "We are not to the marriage point yet."

Renee replied, "Well, the two of you have been dating for two years now." When neither Sam nor Marcus said anything, Renee continued, "We were not talking about you getting married. Stuff, meant that I couldn't believe that Sam was still flying after that crash."

Sam answered her, "The odds of ever being in a plane crash are very high. To be in two crashes, astronomically high."

Marcus said, "I assume it's like a policeman getting shot, some will return to the job, want to get back on the horse. Some will be willing to give it up and at the least not be on the street again."

Renee didn't say anything to what Marcus just said. After a moment, she said, "Sam says you are going to Colorado on your vacation end of July, that right?"

Marcus was quick to answer her, "Yes, but it definitely will not involve flying. What we will do is camping and some hiking. I'd like to see the mountains of Colorado during the summer, not when it's all covered in snow. It will be a laid-back, not be bothered by anyone or anything, just time spent in the sun and fresh air."

"You're not into pot, are you," Renee asked. "Maybe going there for that reason."

"No way. Tried it once in college, didn't care much for it and never tried it again," Marcus replied.

"And Sam said okay to this trip?" Renee asked.

"I said okay on the condition that next year I get to pick the place and it's going to be Italy," replied Sam. "We will spend two days driving to Colorado, do some sightseeing and some outdoor stuff. On the way back, we are going to swing south and stop off at the Grand Canyon. Seen it a lot of times from the air but never up close."

"You are both satisfied with going there after what happened in those mountains?" Renee asked.

"Just like getting back on the horse," Marcus told her.

Renee didn't have anything more to say on the subject, so she excused herself and told them she was going to go inside and check on her husband and Chris and see how the food was holding out.

Sam sat back in the lawn chair and closed her eyes. Marcus sat in the seat Renee had vacated and took hold of Sam's hand. He kissed it and said, "I've been thinking and have a theory that I want to check out."

Without opening her eyes Sam replied, "Theory concerning what?"

Marcus didn't immediately answer her but finally said almost as if he were talking to himself, "Where the money is. At least Agent Beale's."

At the last statement, Sam opened her eyes and looked at him, "And you want to spend our time looking for it?"

"Yes," he answered her. "I've been thinking about it for a while and just now it has become clearer where it might be when Chris went into the pool, at least where to look."

"Where will that be?" she replied. Marcus just smiled at her. "How do you know it hasn't already been found? It's been over two years now," was Sam's response to his statement.

"I called Agent Larson. She told me an extensive search didn't turn up anything," Marcus replied. "Said they went over every inch, about a square mile around where the plane went down with metal detectors and found nothing. They also searched a mile or so around the cabin in all directions in the event that Beale hid it close to the cabin."

"And roughing it in the mountains is how you want to spend your vacation? Our vacation?" she replied.

All Marcus could say was, "Yes."

Sam shook her head a little and said, "You want this city girl to spend a week in the wilderness, fighting off bugs and spiders and wild animals and who knows what else?"

"Sam, Agent Larson said a ten percent reward is being offered for the money found. Could be a lot. It'll be a peaceful vacation in the mountains with a little treasure hunting on the side. It won't be bad, you'll see," he assured her. "A vacation to remember."

Chapter 5

In a room in the Twin Pines Motel was a pile of camping gear and Marcus and Sam were checking it off on a list. There was a tent, sleeping bags, hiking boots, dry food, water, first aid kit, their two carry on suitcases and several rolls of toilet paper. There was a small cooking pot, small frying pan, eating utensils and tin pie pans to serve as dishes. They would try cooking over an open fire, but to be on the safe side, they included a small self-contained butane stove, big enough for one pot or frying pan. And to really be on the safe side, there was a large box of energy granola trail mix bars. Also, Marcus brought along a Coleman lantern, and a flashlight. They were debating whether they should take their rain gear or not. Sam didn't believe that it would take up that much space, so they decided to take it. Marcus held up a small plastic jar and said, "Do not forget to take extra matches." When they had looked over everything, he threw a small folding shovel and an axe in its sheath on the pile. "We have everything the outfitter said we should have for a week. We will wear our jackets; it may be the middle of summer but here in the mountains it is cool in the morning and evenings."

"Aren't you glad we flew to Denver and then rented a car to get here?" Sam said. "Most of this stuff the outfitter who sold it said he'd buy back so it will not be going to California with us."

"No Grand Canyon on the way back though," he said.

"That is the way it goes. Some other time we can see it," was her response.

"I guess so. An ATV rental in the area means we will not have to walk to the cabin. A fifteen-mile walk does not sound like a good start to our vacation, especially carrying all of this gear," he said.

"We're ready here so I'll follow you while you return the SUV and trailer," Sam said.

Marcus shook his head no and said, "No. You stay here in our room. The owner made me rent everything for a week. With all the people coming here and searching for the money last two years it's become common practice to gouge all the fortune hunters. Fewer hunters now. He told me one or two show up every once in a while, so he's got to make as much money as he can. I told him we were only going camping and do some hiking. Couldn't argue him down. I'll pull it to the end of the parking lot and park it there. The assistant night manager said it would be okay. Charged us ten dollars for the week, said nothing about our car. We will just have to leave both here."

When Marcus returned to the room he saw Sam on the bed and looking up at the ceiling. He asked, "You're not having second thoughts, are you?"

"No. Just thinking what we should do on our last night in civilization?' she replied.

"How does have a quick dinner and turn in early sound?" Marcus asked.

She turned on her side so that she was facing Marcus and said, "Why don't we turn in early, then go downstairs and go to that diner and get something to eat?"

At this invitation, Marcus laid down beside her and they kissed. As the kiss lasted longer and longer, they began to undress each other. When they were completely naked they made love as the day turned into the night. Sam stirred and could see light coming through the window and she nudged Marcus awake. "It's morning, we should be getting up. Time to get going," she whispered to him.

He opened his eyes and rolled off the bed and said, "Last time I take your advice."

"Well, we did turn in early and now we are going to get something to eat," she replied with a big smile on her face. "Let's shower, get dressed, have breakfast and pack the ATV. I'm starving. May as well begin to not shave since you won't be doing it in the wild."

They walked the several blocks to a diner. An hour and a half later they had eaten and packed all their equipment on the small trailer that came with the ATV. They stood beside the SUV and its trailer in the parking lot and were studying a map of the area. After a few moments, Sam asked, "Do you know where we are going?"

Marcus began folding the map, stuck it in the ATV saddle bag and said, "Yes, let's go. Put on your helmet the ATV renter provided. Clerk in the motel sold me the map and showed me where to go. He said just head east along the side of this mountain and we should come to a well-used road that the plane investigators and all the money hunters have created. Can't miss it, and if we follow it, it will take us where we want to go. Guy who rented me this showed me how to start it and drive it. We'll go slowly till I get the hang of it."

He started the ATV and Sam got on behind him and they started off. It was easy to find the well-worn trail that the clerk told him about. It looked like a dirt road. They hadn't gone ten miles and Marcus could see that much of the road disappeared, washed out between two mountains, just like the dead prospector had said. They stopped and stared at the washed-out road and Marcus looked around to see how others may have gotten around this obstacle. He saw no other worn area off their road and assumed that everyone traveled over the washed-out area, slowly. He believed he could do the same as others had. Sam was hesitant. Marcus said, "We will take it slow and follow where the road was. Hold on tight. If we go over a slanted area, lean in the opposite direction so that we won't tip over. Picking his way through the washed-out area, after three hundred yards the road reappeared. Shortly they were at the prospector's cabin. Unlike before there was a considerable amount of litter scattered around and civilization's most tell-tale sign, beer cans.

The shelter for the mule had collapsed on one side. The mule's saddle was on the wooden stall rail and the roof rested on it and kept it from completely collapsing. The outside toilet's door hung at a funny angle. It looked like the top door hinge had pulled loose from the wall. Marcus stopped and asked, "Well here it is. Want to go inside?"

Sam looked at it and said, "I don't think so, only fond memory was that I was with you. We came to camp out, so let's camp."

"I have a fond memory too. When we were in it together and I was holding you, was when I became aware that I was falling in love with you. I wondered if you would ever go out with me," Marcus replied.

"All you needed to do was ask," was her reply. "I would have said yes."

"I never told you this, but that Treasury Agent Bale thought of asking you out. Little did I know. I encouraged him," Marcus said.

"I would have told him no," Sam replied with sureness in her voice.

Marcus turned around so that he was facing her. "If we didn't have these helmets on, I'd kiss you." As he turned around, she removed her helmet. He did the same and they kissed. They broke apart, replaced their helmets and he said, "Okay, let's head to where the plane went down and find a place to pitch our tent," Marcus answered.

Sam said, "Let's go in that direction but not to where the crash occurred. Can you find it?"

"We will head to where I remember the helicopters were circling and landing," he replied.

"I hope we can find a nice place near the spot, not the actual spot," was her reply.

"On the map, there is a lake near there. We will take the ATV to it. That is where we are going to go." He drove the ATV on a well-traveled but overgrown road to the place where the plane had crashed. He stopped and they stared. It was gone but from a distance they could see that there were burned remains. Several trees in the area were leafless and charred black. The rock outcropping that the plane had hit showed either paint from the plane or fresh marks where stone had broken away from the impact of the plane. The area looked a lot different in the summer than when it was covered with snow. Neither spoke as they remembered the moment. The ATV renter wanted Marcus to rent their two helmets with microphones and speakers so that they would be able to talk to and hear each other. He thought it would be unnecessary and declined the offer. Marcus believed he could smell the burning fuel mixed with burning flesh and he wanted to move on. After a moment, Marcus started the ATV moving and followed a slight depression as he proceeded to the lake. Neither said anything for the remainder of the ride.

When they arrived at the lake, he stopped the ATV and they looked out over the water. "Oh Marcus. It's beautiful. Let's find a spot near the water." A fish broke the surface for a bug of some sort. "Should have brought along a fishing rod," Sam said as she got off the ATV and Marcus watched her as she walked to the lake's edge.

Sam returned to the ATV and she and Marcus looked around and soon found a grassy area close to the lake where they could camp. Marcus erected their tent and unloaded the ATV trailer. He cleared an area of any flammable material, made a circle of rocks and built a fire. He got a pot of water from the lake, put a water purification tablet that the outfitter sold him in it, and sat the pot between two rocks that would support it over the fire. They ate some of the dry food they carried, and he had a cup of coffee and Sam a cup of cocoa. "I never imagined it could be so pretty and peaceful. Let's go swimming in the lake."

He looked at her and asked, "Did you bring a bathing suit?" He saw her shake her head no and continued. "The lake probably will be quite cold."

"I don't care," she replied. "We can go skinny dipping, there's no one around."

Marcus answered her, "Sounds fine to me. It's a little late. We can do it tomorrow."

"When do we hunt for the money?" she wanted to know. "We are too far from the plane crash."

"So, you are interested in it now. Tomorrow we will start," he answered, "and not at the crash site."

"Where?"

"You will just have to wait and see," Marcus replied.

The next morning after they had eaten, Marcus went back inside of the tent. Sam had cleaned off their breakfast dishes and eating utensils in the lake. She washed out the frying pan and had returned to the tent. "Who would have ever guessed that they made powdered eggs that were this good?" She heard Marcus utter an "ah-hum" from inside the tent. "Where and when do we get started?" she wanted to know.

He moved the tent flap aside and came out of the tent dressed in only a bathing suit. He looked at Sam and said, "Here and now. I'm ready."

In a startled voice, she said, "What!? You did not tell me to bring a bathing suit too? You're going swimming without me?"

"Not going swimming Sam, going treasure hunting," he replied.

She recovered from the surprise that he was in a bathing suit and said, "You believe the money is hidden in the lake?"

"Yes," he replied. "Two reasons. When we were on the plane Beale said if the plane crashed in water, I should buy scuba gear, said it would last for years. Didn't pay much attention to what he was saying."

"But we didn't crash in water!' Sam said.

"No, we didn't," he replied. "Remember when Beale came into the cabin, I said to get the nurse. The first thing she said was to get him out of his wet clothes. Just like at my partner's party when they pulled Chris out of the pool, Regis said let's get you out of those wet clothes."

"Yes, he was wet from the snow he had been crawling in," she replied.

"We assumed that. But, what if he was wet because he had been in water?" was Marcus's next statement.

Sam was listening and had a good question to what she just heard, "It was cold, snowing, and windy. What ever would he be doing in water?"

"Hiding the money Sam, hiding the money he took," he answered. "He would know that it would be looked for. He realized he couldn't get out of here or how far he'd have to walk. I believe that he would have held the suitcase with the money under water and to keep it from possibly floating away would have weighted it down with a big rock or two. Either after or before he decided what to do, he returned to the plane. Either smelled smoke from the cabin or saw the lantern light through the window. We were all gone but he saw enough of our tracks. They hadn't been completely drifted over by then and he was able to follow them or at the least knew which direction we had gone. Follow them until he could see light from the cabin. Where could he put it that would be safe and not found? Come back maybe years later and get it. When asked about his actions, he'd say he didn't take any money especially after he would have learned that it had all disappeared. He had time to come up with a story and would deny our story that he took some or that we misunderstood what he had said. We believed what he told us, he left the group of passengers with a suitcase full of money, but his defense would be that all his training kicked in and he was looking for a way out of here and got lost in the blizzard. Like my question to the treasury agent, how do we, how did he know that it was really on the plane? His defense would again be he never saw it. He was just told it was there."

"And after a year or so, you think he would come back and get it?" she asked.

"Yes. It makes sense," he replied.

"So, you think it's in the lake and you are going to look for it in the water?" she said shaking her head in disbelief.

"When I talked to the Treasury Agent Larson she said that the scoured the area near the crash site mainly in the direction the plane was headed and for over a mile in every direction with metal detectors never found the money nor did they find his gun," Marcus told her.

"If he thought that he could find his way out, going in the direction the plane was headed makes a lot of sense. Remember the nurse said he had been out in the blizzard for almost twelve hours. He could have walked a lot further than a mile. Isn't that the direction we should look?"

"I thought of that and so did Agent Larson. Over the phone she told me they searched almost five miles in that direction and found nothing. If he did head in that direction and as bad as the snowstorm was how could he have found his way back and then the cabin. Our tracks as well as his would have been obliterated and it was dark."

She thought about what he said for a moment before she said, "So you want to look in the opposite direction?"

There was a moment of silence when he replied "Yes," and then asked, "Do I go left or right. I'll start here."

Sam knew that Marcus was serious and said to him, "Remember there were lulls in the snowstorm and he would have been able to see for a moment or two. If I were trying to get out of here the mountains to our left are lower. I'd go in that direction. To our right the mountain looks quite impassable. A big rock juts out of it right down to the water. If he decided he couldn't get beyond it, or he couldn't get out of here, it makes sense that he did back track to the plane and saw our tracks and followed us."

"Okay. I'll go to our right about fifty yards in the event he didn't reach the lake in the same place as we did. I think he would have followed the same depression that we did. It was all downhill. I'll start close to the large rock out-cropping where he knew he could not go around and deep enough until the water is about chest high and just zig-zag down the shore from here," and he stepped to the water's edge.

"Why so deep? If what you said is true, why would he go that far from shore?" she wanted to know.

"I believe the lake would have been lower two months from now and today, deeper because of the snow melt." He picked up a tree branch and broke off the small twigs from it, so it acted like a cane and walked to the water and headed toward the large rock. The next words out of his mouth were, "Christ the water is freezing!" He walked the fifty yards from their camp and went deeper into the lake and began looking. He poked at large rocks that he could see under the clear water and went back and forth toward the shore as he made his way toward where Sam was waiting.

By noon, Marcus had covered the fifty yards he had gone from their camp, came ashore and tried to warm up by their fire. "It's a long shot that he even hid it here. It's just a hunch of yours. Could be he hid it on the other side of the cabin or near where the plane was burning. Dig a hole and cover it up." she said. "Place some sort of marker above it."

"Possible, but remember, how would he dig a hole? The ground wasn't frozen, but he had no way to dig and treasury agents went over the area with metal detectors." Marcus was silent for a moment and said, "We knew where the lake was and came straight here. The ground slanted down to the lake so it would be possible that he angled further to our left and you said the mountains do look lower there. Beale would have just followed the shore of the lake until he realized he couldn't make it, hide the suitcase, follow the lake back to where he started then follow his tracks in the snow, or the smoke from the burning plane, to the plane and then ours to the cabin. Our tracks may have not been totally covered and he knew the direction we went. Began walking until he saw the light from the cabin."

Everything Marcus said made sense and she was silent. Finally, she said, "Well since you are so sure it's in the lake, this afternoon I'll help you look. The two of us will be able to cover much more of the lake," Sam said to him.

That afternoon Sam was down to her bra and panties and thigh deep in the lake. "You weren't kidding when you said the water was cold. I'm freezing," she said between shivering lips.

They covered another fifty yards. Marcus could see that she wasn't looking that much but spent most of her time shivering and continually rubbing one arm and then the other. Marcus angled over to her and said, "Come here." He took her in his arms and held her close. "It's getting late, let's quit for the day. Start again tomorrow. Let's get back to the tent and get you into some clothes and I'll get the fire burning."

Shivering, he guided her to the shore and heard her say, "Maybe I'll let you look by yourself tomorrow. You find it, you can keep my share of the finder's fee."

On the fourth day of looking, Sam said, "You have been looking for four days now, I think you've covered probably a quarter of the lake. Tomorrow will be our last day before we head back to Twin Pines."

"It was only a theory Sam and I've covered several hundred yards, not a quarter of the lake. Tomorrow we will relax, do some hiking and enjoy the scenery," he told her.

The next morning, they were dressed to do some walking. Sam said that they knew what was to the left of their camp and suggested they go to their right to those high mountains. Marcus agreed but believed that they wouldn't be able to get beyond the large rock outcropping that looked like it rose out of the lake at the water's edge. Her reply was that they would climb around it and maybe see some of the country from up high. They started off and within several minutes came to the mountain that they could see in that direction. The rock out-cropping came down to the water's edge and extended into the water several yards. Over the years, the rock had fractured, and pieces had fallen into the lake and were sticking out of the water. Instead of climbing around it, Marcus suggested that since the water was shallow, they try to step on rocks at its base and keep out of the water. He broke off two pieces of broken tree branches and they could be used as balancing canes. They carefully reached the other side of the large rock they saw and discovered it was not part of one big mountain, but there were two mountains, and there was a valley between them. Sam asked, "Where is the cabin from here?"

Marcus looked around and said, "I think it is in the direction of this valley."

Sam with a new sense of interest quickly said, "Marcus, what if we were wrong. Beale didn't go to the left but came this way. In the blizzard, he didn't know which way was up or down, which way led out of here? If the lake were lower it would have been easy for him to walk around that big rock."

Marcus listened to her and replied, "Very possible."

"Maybe if he did come this way at night, would it be possible that he could see the light from the cabin? Smell the smoke?" she wondered aloud.

Marcus was aware Sam's renewed interest of possibly looking for the money in the lake when he asked, "What are you saying? You want to look some more?"

With glee in her voice and a big smile she said, "Why not? Take your clothes off and we will get started."

The two of them stripped down so that they were completely naked, put their clothes in a pile and went to the water. After more than two years he still couldn't stop admiring her beauty and body. He thought that they might make love first, but as soon as his feet hit the cold water any thoughts of love disappeared. Like before they walked in a zig-zag pattern paralleling the shore. Marcus was deeper in the water and Sam stayed closer to shore. They hadn't looked more than five minutes when Marcus peered into the water and believed that he saw something shiny, metal. He yelled to her, "Sam, I think I see something!" She turned to him and saw him go completely under the water and in several seconds, came back to the water's surface. He held up his hand and he was holding an aluminum suitcase. "Sam, Sam, I've found something. I think it's it!" He began to go toward her and then both to the shore. "Rocks were piled on top of it to hold it down," When they reached the shore he sat it down and watched as water trickled from inside and ran down the sides of the suitcase.

Sam was impatient to see what was inside, "Open it! Let's see!"

Marcus released the clasps on the front and more water ran out of the case, but it had an inset lock that kept it closed. Finally, Marcus said, "Let's get dressed and get back to camp. I'll open it with our axe." They got dressed and headed for their camp. When they reached it, he forced the lock out of the case with the axe. Marcus hesitated a moment and then lifted the lid. Inside they could see neatly stacked bundles of hundred-dollar bills. Each was wrapped with a paper band with a denomination on it, $10,000. They both were shocked and didn't say anything for a moment, they just stared. Sam ran her finger across a row and lifted a bundle out.

An hour later they were sitting around their fire and all around them were hundreds of bundles of wet hundred-dollar bills. He asked, "Well, how much?"

"You know I'm not too good in math, but I believe there is four million, two hundred and fifty thousand," she answered. "We will go back later and search for more. He must have taken it and probably hid it too!"

"Whew! Beale wasn't kidding when he said he took a lot," Marcus uttered. If what he said was true, he took one suitcase and hid it. Not the rest of it."

"We'll keep it?" was a statement and a question.

"No," replied Marcus.

"Why not?" she wanted to know.

"I represent the law, it's my duty," Marcus said. "Your half of the finder's reward would be in the neighborhood of two hundred thousand plus. You would be able to open that little boutique shop you've talked about and you could quit flying."

"But you didn't find it as part of your official business. You are just a plain citizen. Are you sure I can't talk you out of it?" Sam asked.

"No," he said, "and don't try. We'll turn it in."

In a moment, she replied, "You're probably right, and ten percent is a lot of money, and if we find more."

It was a statement that Sam believed that they would find more. Later that day they had returned to where they had found the case of money. They looked in the water for about two hours and found nothing. Again, Marcus reminded her that Beale said he took a suitcase full, not all of it. So, they quit looking and returned to their camp site, packed most everything on the trailer in preparation of returning to Twin Pines in the morning.

Chapter 6

They rose early, finished packing and it was just after eleven o'clock in the morning when they arrived at the motel. Marcus had loaded the ATV with its trailer onto the SUV trailer. On the ground in a pile was all their camping gear. Sam was sorting through it and putting it into three piles. She looked up when she saw Marcus approach. "Where did you put it?"

"I put it in the trunk of our car," he said.

Sam wanted to know if it would be safe. "Should be," answered Marcus looking around the parking lot. "Nobody knows about it except us and no one out here except us."

"Okay. This pile," and she pointed to them one at a time, "we return, this one we keep and this one we toss. Let's check in. Make sure the room has a bathtub," she said. "I need to soak in a hot bath." They put all the camping equipment they were going to return in the back of the SUV. Since they had rented it for a week Marcus said they could return it tomorrow.

Marcus checked them in and got their luggage out of storage. After two trips, they carried their keep stuff and their suitcases from storage up to their room and he heard her complain that he should have asked for a ground floor. They piled their toss stuff near a trash can, maybe someone else could use it Sam told him. When he suggested that they eat later and see the town a little he heard her say they could do that after he reported the money. When he tried their cell, he found that it was dead, it hadn't been charged since they left to go camping. He called down to the desk and asked how he could make a long distant call. The man at the check in counter said he would give him an outside line and Marcus called Agent Corry Larson. When he identified himself, she asked, "What can I do for you detective Rothman."

"I found the money Beale took," he said into the phone.

There was a moment of silence when he heard the agent ask, "You found it! How much?"

"Like Agent Beale said, a suitcase full of it. More than four and a quarter million," Marcus told her.

She wanted to know where he was, and he told her the Twin Pines Motel. Ms. Larson instructed him to stay where he was that she would be coming to see him as soon as possible and that he shouldn't tell anyone about what he had found.

Marcus replied, "Who can we tell? I'll be waiting for you." He hung up. The room was silent for a moment when he yelled to Sam, "You still alive or did you drown in there?" He heard a "give me another half hour," so he again called the check-in desk and told the receptionist they would be staying a day or two longer. He again yelled toward the bathroom, "Think if we are going to take all of this camping stuff back, should buy an extra suitcase or mail it."

Downstairs at the check-in counter the receptionist took out his cell and made a call. When he heard hello, he asked, "Mr. Garza?" he heard a grunt that passed for a yes. "You said to call you if I heard anything about people finding money."

The receptionist heard Gino Garza say, "Yeah, wha-da you know?"

"We talked about money for me, that right?" he said into the phone.

Mr. Garza answered him, "Tell me something important and there's a grand in it for you."

The receptionist cleared his throat and said, "A guy and a woman from the plane crash went camping back at the crash. They returned today and the first thing the guy did was ask for an outside line. I hooked him up. Couldn't hear what he said but the number read out was on our motel phone. I checked the area code. It was Washington."

Mr. Garza asked, "What did he say, talk about?"

The receptionist replied, "Like I told you, I couldn't listen in, all I could do was give him an outside line. Then the guy calls me and says he wants to stay a couple of days more."

"Okay," the receptionist heard. "Give me their names and room number. I'll have a couple of my boys check them out."

When Sam got out of the bath, Marcus shaved and took a shower, they got dressed and the two of them went to the nearby diner and got something to eat. Marcus wore his jacket and Sam called him a softie. It was mid-afternoon and they were back in their room. He was in the bathroom brushing his teeth when there was a knock at their door. He heard Sam say that there was someone at the door. "Get it Sam, I'll be right out," he called from the bathroom.

Sam walked to the door and said in a loud voice, "Yes, who is it?"

From the other side of the door she heard, "Government agents, want to talk to Marcus Rothman."

"Just a moment, let me get the door," she replied.

When she opened the door, she saw two well-dressed men. The taller of the two introduced himself as Agent Anthony Jones and his partner Alonzo Shultz and asked if they could come in. Marcus had come out of the bathroom and the introductions were made again. He could see that one of the men was armed. He didn't think much of it since they were treasury agents. After they shook hands, Agent Jones said, "You know why we are here. Where is it?"

Agent Shultz said, "We searched your SUV and found nothing. Is what you found here in your room? I know you didn't check it with the motel security? Did you find it? Where?"

Sam was the first to speak, "You searched our SUV!? You had no right to do that without our permission!"

The two agents didn't have anything to say and for a moment were quiet. Marcus said, "Aren't we going a bit fast here? How did you get here so soon?"

Agent Jones replied, "We're from Denver. Got a call from Washington to meet with you."

Marcus' next question concerned their boss, "When's agent Larson coming?"

"He'll be here as soon as he can get a flight to Denver," agent Shultz said. "Wants you to tell us about the money."

"He!" Marcus said. "I think I need to see some identification."

"No problem," Agent Jones said, and he reached under his jacket and behind his back for his wallet. When his hand come forward it was holding a gun. "Neither of you move! Where did you find it!? Did you take any of the money!? Where is it!?"

Marcus quickly asked, "What money?"

Agent Jones said, "Joey, search the place!" Agent Shultz, now called Joey, began sorting through the camping pile, went to their suitcases, opened them, and scattered clothes around. He opened all the drawers of the dressers in the room and looked under the bed. Agent Jones took out his cell phone and dialed. Marcus and Sam heard him say, "We're upstairs in their room searching. You two stay put," and he closed the phone and put it in his jacket pocket. "Joey, look in the closet and then the bathroom."

When Joey went into the bathroom Marcus said, "He's found it!" Agent Jones turned and looked toward the bathroom and when he did, Marcus knocked the gun out of his hand, and it went flying on the other side of the bed. Before the agent could recover, Marcus hit him knocking him back onto the bed. He grabbed Sam, opened the door, and pulled her through it after him. Joey started to come out of the bathroom, saw what had happened and saw the two motel guests going through the door. He pulled out his gun and quickly fired two shots at them as the door was swinging closed.

In the hallway, Marcus said, "Faster Sam!" as they headed to the exit sign and the stairs. They entered and went down the stairs. Instead of opening the door and rushing through it, Marcus opened it enough to look out. The parking lot was almost empty and beyond it were pine trees on the mountain. He didn't know where the two guys Agent Jones had talked to were, but he made a quick decision. He pushed the door open and the two of them raced across the parking lot. Almost across the macadam he saw a man on a cell phone. He didn't know what he was saying but what went through his mind was, *yes, I see them. They're heading across the parking lot.* He imagined the voice on the other end, Agent Jones saying, *stop them!* Just as they reached the trees he heard three shots fired. The fleeing Marcus and Sam didn't stop. They ran deeper into the forested area and then turned and went west.

Coming through the exit door was Joey. He went to his companions in the parking lot and said, "After them!" and the three ran into the trees.

A minute later Agent Jones was on his cell phone and talking. "Mr. Garza, they made us."

There was a moment of silence when he heard a calm voice say, "Tony, tell me they found the money."

Agent Jones, Tony, answered him, "No. Searched their room and vehicle. Didn't have any."

The phone conversation was not going too well for Tony and he heard a rise in his boss' voice, "Did they say they found it? Know where it is?"

"Not in so many words," Tony replied.

"What da fuck did da say!?" Mr. Garza said into the phone, his voice rising.

"They didn't say that they didn't find it," was the only answer Tony could give in response to his boss.

Mr. Garza was quiet for a moment and seemed to have settled down when he asked, "Where are they now?"

Tony silently breathed a quiet sigh of relief and said, "Took off through the woods. We're looking for them."

"For your sake, I hope you find them, and no shooting. That's all you need is da police there," Mr. Garza said.

Tony didn't know how he was going to say what needed to be said next, so he just told his boss, "Too late Mr. Garza."

Mr. Garza said in an intense under his breath voice, "Which one of you fucking Einsteins decided to shoot dem!?"

Tony could feel the rage through the phone so decided not to try and explain, that could be done later, so he simply said, "Couldn't be helped. You know how irrational Joey can be." He was silent and hoped Mr. Garza would think about what he had just heard and maybe forgive what his nephew had done.

There was no moment of silence before he heard Mr. Garza explode, "Before you found out about da money!? Now police and maybe federal agents will be there!" Then he heard a calmer voice from his boss but with the same intensity, "You idiots better not come back without it! Or them! Or know where it is! Am I clear!?"

"Yes sir, Mr. Garza. No one knows where they went except us. We'll find them," was all that Tony could say and he hoped what he said was true.

There was a moment of silence and he knew better than to hang up on his boss when he heard, "You'd better," and the line went dead.

Chapter 7

Marcus held onto Sam's hand as they ran among the trees and brush. They were both panting as they ran and continued to look back over their shoulders. Finally, they stopped, and he said, "Let's rest. I think we lost them. Maybe we should have just stayed there and denied finding any money?" They sat on the pine needle forest floor when Sam asked, "Who were those guys?"

"I don't know," replied Marcus. "They definitely were not treasury agents. Didn't know that Larson was a woman and not a man and one was armed. Saw the bulge on his shoulder. You saw how serious they were. They believed we had found some or all of the money. Do believe their next step would have been to torture us."

"How did they know we found the money?" Sam asked. When Marcus didn't answer her, she asked, "Who we were? Were we found it? Were they could look for more? We didn't see or talk to anyone except the motel receptionist when you checked in. You tell him?"

"No. All I did was call Washington, but I was in our room," said Marcus. "Couldn't have been overheard. Might be possible the check-in clerk listened in to the phone call somehow, but all he did was get me an outside line."

They were silent for a while when Sam said, "They knew who to ask for. Somehow, they knew who we were, at least who you were."

"A better explanation would be that someone in Washington found out, maybe Larson told people or was overheard telling someone. They, or he, called someone in Denver and told them, told him who we were and where we were. Only immediate explanation I can come up with, why they found us so quickly and that we had found some of the money. Whoever they were, they weren't treasury agents."

They were both quiet and Sam asked Marcus with expectation in her voice, "What are we going to do?"

Marcus' immediate answer was, "Somehow we need to get to a phone or the police." He did not say how they were going to do it.

Sam's follow up question was, "Can we go back?"

"No. I don't think so. You saw how desperate they were. They were willing to shoot us. As a detective, I believe that at least one of them will be watching the motel and right now the others are still looking for us."

"You're probably right," Sam said. Then she asked, "Do you think they will give up?"

"Don't know," he said. "Maybe they don't know if we found some of the money or how much, but if they do, four and a quarter million are a lot of reasons to keep searching. Or they might think that we know where the money is and will want us to tell them."

"What makes them believe we know anything about the money, where it is?" she asked.

"If they somehow found out we found a suitcase of it, means we know where the rest of it is," Marcus replied.

After a moment, Sam said, "But we don't know where the rest of it is Marcus, I'm afraid." After a moment's hesitation, she asked, "Which way should we go?"

Not sure he said, "We will keep walking in this direction. We'll eventually have to run into a road or someone."

In another part of the pine forest the four gangsters were looking for the two fleeing motel guests. Joey suggested they split up in order to cover more territory.

"Keep in sight so we don't get lost or whistle so we know where everyone is," Tony told the others. "Marco, you go back and keep an eye on the motel in case the show up there. Remember, no more shooting!"

As Marco walked in the direction of the motel, Joey asked Tony, "Was uncle Gino really mad?"

As Tony watched Marco turn, head toward the motel and was out of ear shot, he said, "Don't ask. But if we don't find them, maybe we shouldn't go back to Denver." He was quiet when he heard Joey begin with the next question but before he could get it out Tony said, "He's your uncle. You know better than anyone how irrational and violent he can be."

"Yeah, let's keep looking. It'll be dark soon," said Joey. A half hour later, not far from where the three gangsters were walking, Marcus heard a short loud whistle. The two listened and heard an answering sharp short whistle. Marcus said, "That is not a bird. I think I hear them! Look for a place to hide! We are too tired to try and out run them."

"How about under that rock over there," she said and pointed.

When they got to it they found the rock was part of a ledge and formed a natural overhang. They got under it and as far inside as they possibly could. "Keep quiet," Marcus whispered. They were quiet and didn't hear one of the men pursuing them, reach and stand above them on the rock. In a moment, a second pursuer approached the one on the rock and they could hear one of them ask, "See anything?"

"Naw," a second of them answered. "Pretty rocky in this area over here. Let's swing to our right and catch up with Benny and mosey back to the motel and keep an eye out there. They don't know where to go except back to the motel."

They were not sure which one said that he had seen a deer, did that count. Then one of them yelled to Benny that he should wait up. They were coming to him. They heard one of them say to wait a sec, he needed to take a leak. Shortly over the rock Marcus and Sam could see a stream of water.

They waited and everything swas silent. After five minutes Marcus whispered, "I think they've gone."

"How far do you think we've come." she asked.

Marcus said, "Couple of miles at least."

She wanted to know. "What are we going to do? It's getting dark."

Marcus thought a moment and said, "I think I can find our way back to the motel. We headed west, so all we got to do is head east. Circle the mountain. We won't go up or down. But you heard them, we can't take a chance that those guys won't be there waiting for us. Problem is, the sun has gone behind the mountain, so after a while we won't know if we are going east or not. I've heard all those stories, true or not, that lost people tend to walk in circles. It's chilly but maybe our best bet will to find a place to stay the night and start back tomorrow."

Still skeptical, Sam asked, "And tomorrow?"

All that Marcus could say was, "We will worry about tomorrow, tomorrow."

Back at the motel Tony and his three accomplices stayed in the pine trees and could see three police cars at the motel entrance. It was beginning to get dark so they could see several policemen looking over the driveway and parking lot with flashlights. "We better move to the far end of the parking lot before they come into the woods looking for us," he said. At the middle of the parking lot the four wondered out of the forest and joined about twelve other motel guests looking at the police and watched what they were doing. Tony waved his three companions to the side when he was sure that the group of on-lookers were sure that they were part of the group. When he felt that they were far away from the group so as not to be heard he whispered, "Marco, you and Benny head for Benny's car. Me and Joey will go to his SUV, pull out and meet you at the entrance of the motel. Act casual and continue to look at the police and stare at them. Whatever you do, don't attract attention!"

Tony and Joey got in Joey's SUV and drifted out of the parking lot. Tony said, "If treasury agents are coming from Washington, they won't get here until at the earliest tomorrow afternoon." Joey didn't say anything, and Tony was silent for a moment. "And now police! God damn it anyway! We can't look for them now anyway, too dark."

Joey asked, "You think they will come back here to the motel?"

"Don't know," said Tony. "If they do we cannot challenge the police or try and take them away from them."

"What do you think we should do then?" Joey wondered out loud.

Tony didn't answer him. Instead, when they got close to Benny's car, Tony took out his cell and dialed. Joey heard him say, "Marco, remember that seedy looking motel we passed coming into town, the Winds. We are going to meet up there in about two hours, tell Benny to check us in and then stay put. In the meantime, we're going to drive slowly up and down nearby roads. Maybe we'll get lucky. You get out and check into this motel, keep an eye on the motel and police in case they show up so we can quit looking. Receptionist asks about why no car, tell her your brother dropped you off while he went into town to see an old girlfriend. If she asks, your luggage is in his car. Whatever Benny does, no more shooting!" Tony closed his cell and stuck it in his pocket. "That goes for you too, Joey!" he said. "Maybe I otta take your gun from you?"

Much deeper into the pine forest Sam said to Marcus, "Let's rest for a second."

"This looks like as good a spot as any other," he said. "We'll stop here. There is a slight hollow between those rocks. There is a lot of pine needles that will make the ground softer and it's getting too dark to look for anywhere better. Hopefully if it gets windy the rocks will protect us. I'll take my jacket off and try to cover the both of us as best as I can. Help me feel around for any rocks that we would lie on." They cleared out any rocks that they could feel and they laid down. Marcus took Sam in his arms and held her close.

"I can see the moon every once in a while when it peeks from behind the clouds," Sam whispered to him.

"Well with the moon we know which way is east," he replied.

"It's so pretty and peaceful here with the wind whispering through the pines. I wouldn't have believed how nice it is in the mountains of Colorado if I didn't witness it for myself," she said.

"Better forget about how nice it is and get some sleep. I know you're tired and tomorrow could be another exhausting day," was all that he could say. Shortly he could hear the even breathing of Sam.

Marcus didn't know how long they had been asleep. He could feel her shaking him and whispering into his ear, "Marcus, wake up."

He was quickly alert. *Was it possible the men looking for them had somehow found them,* raced through his mind? Just as quietly, he whispered to Sam, "What is it?"

"Ssssh. Be quiet," she whispered. "I heard something. I think they've found us."

Marcus held her close and both were quiet. If it were true, there wasn't too much they could do. Most likely it would be too dangerous to go running when they couldn't see anything. Marcus listened but all he could hear was the wind through the pines. He looked around and didn't see the light beams from flashlights. They couldn't be searching for them. After a moment, he whispered, "We're both a little jumpy. I don't hear or see anything. It must have been the wind. I think we should go back to sleep."

He settled back and could feel her put her arms around him. He just closed his eyes when she whispered, "There it is again! Ssssh. She sat up and pointed, "Over there, I saw something move!"

Marcus joined her in a sitting position and stared in the direction he could see her point. The half-moon broke out from behind the clouds and along a rock ledge he saw a mountain lion. He believed it was stalking them. He moved a little out of their pine needle bed and found a heavy branch. He broke it until it was about the size of a baseball bat. "Stay here," he said. "I'm going to try and scare it off."

He heard her say, "Be careful, please. It could be dangerous."

Marcus ran as best as he could over the rocky ground in the direction of the rock ledge, all the while yelling at the cat. "Get cat! I'm going to get you! Scram! Here I come! If your smart, you'll take off! I'll beat your ass with my club!" When he reached the rock ledge where he though the cat was he began to beat the rocks with the club. He believed that the cat did, in fact leave, even though he was unable to see it. He returned to Sam. "I think we will be okay. I hope it took off *pronto*!"

"What if it comes back," she asked.

To soothe her fears, he said, "I don't think it will come back. To be safe I'll stay awake and keep an eye open."

Soon they were in their embracing position and he could hear her soft even breathing. He tried to stay awake but after a while he drifted off also.

At the new motel, the Winds Motel, where the three men had stayed, it was just beginning to get light out and Tony was up. He got the other two men moving. "Time to get going and find those two. It's light enough to see."

Joey asked, "We going back into the woods?"

Tony looked at him and said, "And do what. We don't have a clue where they are or are headed. They didn't make it back to the motel and Marco is still there."

"Maybe they got lost. Spent the night in the forest," Joey replied.

"If we are not going into the woods, where are we going to look?" asked Benny. "What if we get lost? We're no boy scouts. Probably easy to happen, get lost."

Tony listened to what Benny said. "I agree. Instead of going into the trees, we'll continue what we started last night."

"What's that?" asked Joey and Tony saw both of his companions look at him for an answer. There was no doubt in either of their minds that Tony was in charge.

He waited a moment as if he were thinking before he answered. "We will drive around on some of the back roads near the motel. Let's hope they walk out onto a road and we find them. Let's stop at that McDonalds at the edge of town and grab some breakfast and coffee. I'll go with Benny. Joey, you'll be by yourself in your SUV. Any questions?" His two companions were quiet and when they didn't answer him, he said, "Okay, let's get going."

It was beginning to get light out. Marcus was awakened by several birds calling to each other. He tried to stretch but found it difficult with Sam's arms around him. His stirring woke her. She tried to wipe sleep from her eyes when he said, "Time to get up and out of here."

Sam arose and asked, "Which way?"

Marcus looked around and said, "Not sure. Looking for a place to sleep we turned around a couple of times and with this fog that's rolled in, I'm not sure which way is east. It's cloudy, no sun. Let's just start walking and hope it is not in circles and it's back to the motel."

"What if those guys are still there?"

"I'm sure the police were called after the shooting and I believe we would be safe. Once we are close I'll look around and make sure before we go into the motel."

Standing beside him she was ready to begin walking and at the end of his last statement she added, "Or is it going to rain? Hear that? Sounds like thunder."

"Can't tell where it's coming from, but it probably would be from the west," he answered her. He was not sure which direction the rock ledge pointed but following it was as good a bet as any other. They had gone two hundred yards when Marcus reached down and broke off a chunk of tree branch and he gave it to Sam. He picked up a second piece for himself and used it as a cane.

She commented to him, "I don't really need a walking stick."

He replied, "Hang onto it, you might need it."

She stopped and looked at him with a question on her face, "Huh? Why do you think that? We can't fight those guys off with tree branches."

Without looking away he said to her, "That mountain lion is still stalking us."

That statement got her attention and she looked around. "What? Where? I don't see it. What makes you think that?"

"He's over there to our left. I see him every once in a while. I want us to be ready as we can be if he decides that one of us should be breakfast."

Marcus reached out and took her by the hand. "You lead. He attacks, go for his eyes."

"How do you know it's a he?" she asked.

"Okay, I don't know. Maybe it's a her. Doesn't much matter," he replied. "Let's go over this hill instead of going around it."

After they had walked ten minutes' Sam asked, "I haven't seen that lion. You think he's still following us?"

"I don't know but hang onto your stick just to be safe."

"I think it's going to rain Marcus. It's getting darker and the thundering is getting louder. Maybe we should look for a place where we can get out of it if it does rain," she said. "Can we rest for a while?"

"Okay to both, we will rest and look for a place where we won't get so wet if it does rain," he replied.

In Benny's car Tony was on his phone. "What is it Joey?" he asked into the phone.

In his SUV Joey said, "Ya know, driving around I've passed a couple of dirt roads off the highway. Maybe I should check these out. What da you think?"

Tony thought about it for a moment and replied, "Why not. Don't drive too far and for Christ sake don't you get lost or stuck! Where are you now?"

Joey replied, "About two miles past the bridge on 42. I'll be going north."

Back at the Twin Pines police station Agent Larson showed her credentials and said, "Thanks for seeing us Sergeant Wilson. I'm Corry Larson, agents Jeff Turner, Mike Myers and Irving Plank." The sergeant shook everyone's hands and said, "No problem. Good to see you again. I remember you from the plane crash and then the search for the money. You remember Sheriff Tillman here."

The sheriff said, "Good to see you again Ma'am," and they all shook hands again. "What can we do for you?"

"I received a call from one of the plane's passengers who returned to the site. He called me, said he found some of the money," she said. "Checked with the motel and found out he and his wife or girlfriend were the ones involved in the shooting there."

Sergeant Wilson replied, "Me and two deputies investigated when the sheriff called. With help from the desk clerk, she told us what she believed happened. She came on duty after the shooting had occurred. Went to their room and found where a bullet had hit their door and a second one in the wall outside their door. Believed that they were shot at as they fled the room. Two witness in the motel told us they saw the two flee into the trees and then two men we believed were with the shooter also shot at them. The original shooters joined them and they went into the trees after the man and woman."

"The woman, as best that I know, is his girlfriend. How many shooters were there?" Agent Turner asked.

"Depending on which witness you talked to, there were either three or six," was the sergeant's reply.

"Any of the witnesses say the saw anyone carrying a metal case?" Ms. Larson asked.

"No," answered the sergeant, "But again they were not asked that question. I called in for more help and five of us searched the woods to the east for both until it got dark. Found neither the victims nor the shooters. Searched their room, found a few camping items, clothes scattered around and that was it. Thought it might have been a foiled robbery. We did not know any of the particulars, had no idea about the money but now it all makes sense. Why didn't they call us and report the money, maybe bring it in?"

Ms. Larson said, "He called me and told me they had found it. I never told him to take it to you but said I'd be there in a day. Thought that we could deal with it then. But now, we need your help sheriff and any men you can spare. We must find them! They either have some of the money or may know where it is."

The sergeant said, "How do we know that the shooters didn't catch up to them in the woods and have them. Could be they forced our victims to tell where they found it, want to keep them quiet so they can go and get the rest. They know where it is, maybe wait a long time before they return to get it."

"A good theory, but I have to assume that they didn't find them," replied Ms. Larson. "The two of them are out there and are lost. I suggest we look for them until we either find them or come up with evidence that the shooters have taken them as prisoners."

After a ten-minute rest, Marcus decided it was time to move on and they began to walk.

They had walked for a half hour when Sam said, "Marcus! Is this the same rock ledge we were walking by before! Have we just made a big circle!?"

"I don't believe so Sam. What's the matter?" he asked.

"Nothing, I'm just tired and hungry. Let me lean against these rocks for a while. I'll be alright," she said in a tired voice.

"We need to find some shelter. The wind has picked up and I can feel rain in the air," as he pulled her away from the rock and he urged her forward.

"I'm so tired Marcus, can't we rest longer? Just let me catch my breath," she said.

"I'll help you, lean on me," and he took her arm tried to put it around his shoulder. She pulled away from him and began to walk.

From behind the rocks the mountain lion leaped and landed on Marcus' back. The lion tried to hold him as its rear paws wrapped around the side of his stomach, Front claws digging into his lower chest. Its jaws grabbed at his neck and shoulder on his left side. They both fell to the ground. All that he could say was, "Aaaaah! Sam help!"

Sam turned and saw what had happened. She lifted the tree branch she had been using as a cane to help her walk and swung hard at the lion. She caught it on its back. It snarled through its closed jaws and lifted a paw as if to strike at her. Neither were very effective. It kept a firm grip with one paw around Marcus and a tight grip on his shoulder near his neck. If he was not so tired, Marcus might have been able to fight the lion off, at the least, get away from it. Sam's second swing was harder and hit the cat on its head. It let go of Marcus and assumed a pouncing posture. She believed she would be its next victim. Marcus was able to turn over onto his back and quickly reached out with his right hand and grabbed the mountain lion by its jaw. He folded its lip into its mouth so that it was across the cat's teeth. It tried to bite his hand but when it closed its mouth the harder it bit Marcus' fingers, the deeper it was biting into its lip. It tried to back away but Marcus kept a firm hold on its jaw so it was pulling him at the same time. The lion was unable to pull him very far. Instead of swinging at the cat again, Sam began to poke at its eyes with her makeshift cane. It tried to pull back further but the weight of Marcus made that impossible. Finally, Marcus let go of the cat's jaw because the cat's teeth may have been biting into its lip, but also it was biting into Marcus' fingers. He was sure that it soon would be able to break his fingers. The lion had enough. It turned and bounded off. When it did Marcus laid back and closed his eyes.

Almost immediately he heard, "Marcus! Marcus! Open your eyes! Tell me you're alive!"

Without opening his eyes, he said, "I'm alive, but it hurts a lot."

"Thank God you're okay," she said. "Let me help you up." When he was sitting, she offered, "I'll help you get your jacket and shirt off and see how bad it is. They're both torn to shreds and your neck is bleeding."

"I think it's bad Sam. I can feel the blood running down my chest and my left arm is numb, difficult to move without a lot of pain. I think it may have broken a finger on my right hand and it's bleeding a lot."

With his jacket and shirt off she said, "It's bad Marcus. I think you'll live though. Teeth just missed puncturing your carotid artery. The bite looks deep. It's not bleeding as bad as you think. The claw marks look as bad as the bite, maybe worse." She tore off a piece of his shredded shirt. "Here, wrap this around your finger."

"Put my shirt over the worse wound." As she was doing what he asked, he was removing his belt. "Put my belt around my chest to hold my shirt tight against the scratches and then help put my jacket back on, just wrap it around my shoulders. I can't get my arm through the sleeve. Just tie them together." When she had done what he asked, he staggered, tried to rise. "Help me up, we have to get going."

He stood with her help and she asked, "Are you sure that you can go on? Maybe we should wait a while? We both need a rest."

"What other options do we have?" was all that he could say.

She took his right arm and put it over her shoulder, "Lean on me. I'll help you," she said, and they started off.

In the Twin Pines Motel Sergeant Wilson said that witnesses thought that the fleeing man and woman headed east when they entered the forest. He said he has called for additional help, sheriff deputies, rescue volunteers and a state police helicopter. He had also called for help from the state police and was told they would help. They would get search dogs from Durango, but they wouldn't get here before tomorrow.

Agent Turner asked, "What should we do, don't know the country but want to help."

His companion Agent Meyer said, "Nor are we dressed for the bad weather that seems to be headed our way."

The sheriff said, "We will drop you off on some of the roads west of here, on the chance that they got turned around and got lost and headed west. Our best searchers and the helicopter will go east. I will provide you with boots and rain gear. We definitely don't want you to get lost. Don't get off the roads and we will pick you up later. Call out to them every once in a while."

Sergeant Wilson said, "Okay, if there are no more questions or concerns, let's get started."

In the forest, Marcus was leaning on Sam and the two of them walked slowly. Marcus was shuffling along and trying to keep up with

Sam. They both were startled by the loud thunder that seemed to be close by. Marcus said, "Thunder is closer. We're going to get rain. No place to go."

Sam replied, "Don't worry about it. Next big pine tree or rock overhang we come to. We're going to park it and hope we don't get too wet."

The police helicopter pilot said to Sheriff Tillman in the sheriff's command center, "Can't go up sheriff. A big storm is moving in and poor visibility. It's already beginning to rain. Mountain updrafts are too dangerous to fly in."

"The storm clouds have made it too dark to see well and they will bring on night sooner. It'll be too dark in another hour or so. Have to call off the search for today," he said.

Ms. Larson asked, "What can we do? What's next?"

"All we can do under the circumstances, is call everyone back and pick up your agents. If the weather breaks, first light tomorrow we will start again," said the sheriff. The helicopter pilot said he would go up as soon as the weather permits. Plus," added the sheriff, "tomorrow the dogs will get here. Don't know if they will be any help. The rain will have washed away any scent that they might have been able to detect."

Ms. Larson didn't hold out much hope for using the dogs. "You're probably right, the rain will have washed away any chance of them picking up their trail."

Sergeant Wilson agreed but added, "At least there is a chance."

"Wherever they are I only hope that they can find shelter," Ms. Larson said.

Drops of water were falling on the two as they continued to flee. Sam struggled to keep Marcus on his feet and moving. "There, that big tree, let's go to it. Maybe we won't get so wet. Marcus, you are shivering."

"Sam, I'm so cold," he uttered.

"Hold onto me tighter, I'll try and keep you warm."

"My neck and shoulder are hurting more. The numbness has worn off," he whispered to her.

Rain was hitting the window of the sheriff's office and occasionally, lightning lit up the outdoors. "Sandy, our dispatcher, just told me that everyone has checked in. No luck," Sergeant Wilson told the group.

"I pray they are okay and we find them tomorrow. I need a ride back to the motel," Ms. Larson said to no one in particular.

I'll drive you," said Sergeant Wilson, "and Sandy said all there of your agents have been dropped off there."

Sam was leading Marcus to the large pine tree when she said, "Marcus, what's that?"

"It looks like the roof of a building. Let's go," he said and helped her as she pulled him along. As the two moved as fast as Marcus could go, in forty steps they were out of the forest and into a clearing. Across a weed overgrown road, they saw an abandoned mining operation. Rusted machinery littered the area and several of the buildings were leaning to their side. Windows that could be seen were either broken out, discolored, or boarded up. Fifty yards from the buildings they could see the mine shaft and it looked like a door of metal bars went across it. When they reached the buildings, it began to rain harder.

Sam pulled Marcus to what looked like the biggest and least sagging of the buildings and urged him inside. The door was hanging at an angle and from one hinge. She pulled it far enough so that they could enter. It was an office at one time. A deserted desk, and a broken swivel chair were in the room. The floor was littered with old papers and a slanted bulletin board seemed to hang precariously behind the desk. Dust and spider webs were everywhere. "It's dirty and for the most part dry. We will stay out of the area that looks like it's leaking," she said after they were inside. She took a moment and tried to pull the door so that it was closed more.

Marcus sat on the floor and said, "It'll be nice to rest."

Sam couldn't believe that he was tired. He always seemed so full of energy and to her he seemed tireless. In the fading daylight, she looked at him and saw a pale face. She touched his head. "Your forehead is hot! You have a fever." She untied his jacket sleeves and began to take the jacket off his shoulder. "I want to look at your wounds."

"Easy Sam, don't make me bend my arm," he said to her.

"I can't see it too well but appears to be all red and I can see puss oozing out of the neck wound," she said to him. "Your finger has stopped bleeding," she added.

He tried not to alarm her so in a calm and quiet voice he said, "That means it's infected. Don't worry about it. Let's get comfortable and get some sleep."

Chapter 8

Sometime during the night the rain had stopped. The sun was just clearing the mountains and Sam heard birds singing. She nudged Marcus and asked, "Did you hear that?"

He tried to answer her but was not clear, "Wha, wha… is Sam?"

She was quick to reply, "I think I heard something."

"Canna'… hear," he was able to say.

She turned and looked at him. He looked flushed. His face had a definite reddish tint to it. Concern was in her voice when she said, "You're mumbling." She put her hand to his forehead and said, "You're burning up. Just lie there. Somehow, someway I'm going to have to get help. There it is again! I can hear someone calling, I hear them calling your name! Someone has found us!" Sam rose and went to the door, pushed it open further and yelled. "Here! Here! We're in here!" Standing in the doorway she could see someone hurrying to her. When he was close enough, she recognized him, but didn't remember his name. He interviewed her after the crash and asked questions about the missing money.

He went up the two steps of the building. "Jesus, we've been looking for you everywhere, police and volunteers. Thought you went east, not west."

"Help me. He's hurt and can't get up!" she said to the treasury agent.

Agent Turner said as he entered the building, "I'm with the treasury department, Jeff Turner, do you remember me?"

Sam shook her head and said, "Yes"

"What happened to him? Was he shot?" the agent asked.

"No," Sam was quick to answer. "He was attacked by a mountain lion."

Agent Turner went to Marcus, knelt and asked, "Mr. Rothman, can you hear me? Can you say anything?" There was no answer. The agent said, "Looks bad. Think he's unconscious."

Sam said to him, "He has been mumbling. He has a high fever. I looked at the bite last night and think that it is infected! He has been slipping in and out of consciousness, maybe he's delirious"

"Sounds bad," Agent Turner said to her.

"Can you help me? Help him?" she asked.

Agent Turner pulled Marcus' jacket away from his shoulder and looked at the lion bites. They looked healed over but were red and swollen. Agent Turner felt around them and could see white puss oozing from them. The scratches on his chest looked bad but were not swollen. He replaced Marcus' jacket over him as best he could. The next thing he did was feel for a pulse. When he found one, he next touched Marcus' forehead. He looked at her and replied, "He's alive but he's burning up. You're right. The bites are infected and he needs medical attention, the scratches need to be stitched closed, more than anything I can do for him. We are trained for accidents, stopping the bleeding from stabs or gun shots, how to deal with people that have heart attacks, people in shock, but not how to deal with infections." He took out his cell phone and said, "I'm calling for help. He surely can't walk out of here." He punched in some numbers and said, "Damn it!"

To his remark, she had to ask, "What is it?"

"Battery is dead. No signal. I'll hike back out to the main road, get help and get right back to you." He turned to go and said, "Ms. Larson said you called and said you found some of the money. Was that true?"

"Yes," she answered. "Marcus believed it was the money the agent on the plane took and hid."

"We searched your SUV and room, checked with the motel baggage storage area, found nothing. Where'd you put it?" he asked.

"We rented a car in Denver, a light blue Ford Taurus, and drove to Twin Pines. Marcus locked the money in the trunk. Keys would be in my purse in our motel room," she told him.

"And the car is in the parking lot?" Agent Turner asked.

"Should be. We didn't move it and Marcus said the money would be as safe there as anywhere else. No one knew about it," was all that she could say.

"I'll be damned," Agent Turner said. Then as he headed for the door he said, "Just sit tight. Stay with him. I'll be back with help as soon as possible," and she could see him hurrying through the doorway and start off at a brisk pace.

Sam didn't know what she could do for Marcus, so she just held him and whispered encouraging words that help was on the way. Then she threatened him, telling him that he didn't dare leave her. Sam didn't know how seriously he had been hurt and now he was unconscious. She thought that hours had passed but only ten minutes when she thought that she heard a vehicle. She didn't know that it was approaching in the opposite direction that Agent Turner had gone. She now said to Marcus, that she knew that he was hurting but to just hang on for a few minutes more. Help was here. "I can hear them." Without getting up she yelled, "Here! Here! We're in here!"

The door of their building cautiously opened and Joey entered the building with his gun out. He took a quick look around the empty room, saw that it was empty except for the two of them. He waved his gun threateningly and said, "Well, well. Look at who we got here. Both of you get up! We're leaving!" and his hand went out to grab Sam.

Sam recognized that the man in front of her was one of the men from back at the motel. She quickly moved out of his reach. He then focused on Marcus and repeated his demand. "Get up!"

Sam said, "He can't get up. He's hurt bad!"

Joey took a step closer to where they were and looked down at Marcus. "Don't try anything funny," he said addressing both. "Try something and I'll shoot you!" Again, he said in a louder more forceful voice, "Get up!" When Marcus didn't move, Joey grabbed the jacket and pulled it off Marcus. He could now see the swollen and red bite wounds. Joey kicked out and caught Marcus on the side. Marcus didn't respond to the kick. Joey was close to them both and now pointed the gun at Sam. "Lady, tell me, you find the money? Where is it!?" She didn't say anything. He pointed his gun at Marcus and shouted, "I'll shoot him right here you don't tell me!"

Sam looked him in the eye and said in no uncertain terms, "I don't know where it is. What we found, he hid, back at the crash site. Didn't tell me where. Shoot him and you'll never find it."

She could see Joey think about what she said to him. Saw him hesitate a moment, take out his cell phone and punch in some numbers. He said into the phone, "It's me. I found them." There was a pause and he again spoke into his phone, "He appears to be hurt. Maybe unconscious. She says they did find money, but he hid it. She don't know where. Said it's somewhere back at the crash site." These last words were followed by several "yeahs" and then, "I don't know where I'm at. Somewhere off of thirty-one." There was another pause before she heard, "Right, I'll get back on the main road and head for town. Meet you at our motel." He put his phone away, tucked his gun in his belt and bent down and grabbed a hold of Marcus right arm and lifted and pulled him toward the door. He kept his hand near his gun when he said to her, "I'm taking him to my car, don't try anything. I'll kill the both of you, you hear!?"

Sam got on the other side of Marcus and helped Joey carry and drag him to the black SUV on the dirt road. Joey opened the rear door and helped Sam put Marcus on the seat. She got in beside him. The movement had caused the scratches to open up and he began to bleed. Joey got in, started the SUV, turned around and headed down the road and back toward town.

Several minutes later Joey pulled into the parking lot of the Winds Motel and parked beside Benny's car. Before he could get out of the SUV, Tony opened the rear door, grabbed Sam by the arm and said, "Out!" He held her arm and said to Benny, "Put her in the front seat!" Benny grabbed her other arm, opened the front passenger side door of the SUV and forced Sam in. "Hold her Joey."

"Benny, other side," said Tony. Benny slid onto the seat of the SUV and got beside her. Tony got into the back seat beside Marcus. When they were all settled in, Tony reached toward the front and grabbed Sam by the hair and pulled her head toward him. "I don't believe your friend here would have hid the money and not tell you where." Sam struggled but Tony had a firm grip on her hair and her head was pulled back against her seat. "You found it! Where is it!?" Sam was quiet. "How much did you find!? Where you'd find it!?" Tony pulled her head tighter against the seat. Sam squirmed but couldn't free herself. "Tell me!" he shouted. "I'm gonna hurt you, you don't!"

She struggled and fiercely got the words out, "I'd have to show you."

"How much did you find?"

"Over four million. Take us to a hospital first. Then I'll tell you, and only then."

"Whew!" Tony said. "We gotta get that money! Tell me where at the crash site he hid it!"

Sam remained silent.

Joey in the front seat said, "And we should trust you!? Why? I don't believe a damned word you say. Let me Tony, I'll make her talk."

"Shut up Joey," Tony said from the back seat.

At her comment, Tony relaxed his grip on her but still held her so she could not get away. "A treasury agent found us before you did. I told him where it was and he now is going after it," she said to Tony still holding her hair in the back seat.

"So, it's not at the crash site. And we should believe that bull shit story!" said Joey. "Why didn't he take you? I didn't see any other car coming down that road and for sure I didn't pass anybody walking!"

"Think back," she said. "You remember seeing muddy footprints going through the door." She waited a moment so that Joey could try and picture in his mind what he had seen if she were being truthful. She pressed on, "He was walking, went opposite direction you drove us. You wouldn't have seen him. He will take a while to walk back, but he's going to tell about the money before he comes back to get us. If you want to beat him to it, you'd better hurry. Get us to a doctor or a hospital."

After he heard what she said, Tony spoke up, "We saw that sign, hospital and an arrow pointing when we were coming into town, head for it Joey. Joey put the SUV in gear and started driving to where they had seen the hospital sign. They reached it and found the two-story hospital was only three blocks from the sign. Joey pulled in near the entrance and stopped. "I'll keep her here, you two take the guy in and make it fast!" Tony said.

Benny got out and so did Joey. The wrestled Marcus from the back seat and placed one of his arms over each of their shoulders. They walked him in. "You better not be bull shitting us bitch. You're lying, I swear I'll kill you myself," Tony said to Sam. In a moment she could see Benny and Joey returning to the SUV. They got in and they quickly left the hospital lot. When they had gone several blocks, Joey said, "Dropped him off, parked him on a chair and left before anyone could ask questions."

"Okay lady, let's have it," Tony demanded.

"Let me out first," she said.

Tony who had a hold of her hair the whole time pulled her head back and asked, "You don't trust us?"

Barely above a whisper they heard, "No."

Tony pulled her head back further, "Let's have it! We took your boyfriend to the hospital!" he said to her.

"It was in the lake. What we found is in the trunk of our car at the motel," she told them. "A blue Taurus, keys are in my purse in our room."

"We thought you drove an SUV," Joey said.

"Only here in Twin Pines, rented it," she replied.

Tony took out his cell phone and punched in some numbers. She heard Tony ask, "Can you see a blue Taurus in the motel's parking lot?" There was a lull in the conversation for a moment before she heard, "What is the chance you can get back in her room and look for the car's keys?" After a short pause, Tony continued talking, "See if you can hot wire it and not be noticed, drive it back to our motel. We'll meet up with you there," and he hung up. "Pull over Joey." When he stopped, Tony let go of her hair and said, "Let's wait for about five minutes. Give Marco time to get the car." They just sat there in silence. After a while, Tony said, "I've been straight with you lady, hope you're telling the truth. Sorry about what happened back at the motel. Now I want you to promise you will give us at least twenty minutes before you call the police. Promise me and I'll let you out."

"I promise," she replied to Tony's request.

"Hope your boyfriend's okay. Get out." Tony said as he let go of her hair.

As soon as she was out of the SUV, she watched it drive off and quickly turned around and headed back toward the hospital. Within five minutes she got to the hospital and entered. At the reception desk the woman looked up at her and asked if she could help her. Sam said, "I'm with the guy just brought in with the infected bite marks." The receptionist told her to wait, she will get someone to talk to her. She dialed a number and spoke into her headset. In a moment, a nurse approached and took Sam's arm and guided her into a small office.

"I'm the admittance nurse. Your friend is in the emergency room. Doctor Lee is working on him right now. I can't tell you much more until after he is admitted. I would like some background information on him, you and how it happened," the nurse said. "First question is about his insurance. Does he have any?"

"Yes, but I don't know with which insurance company. Check in his wallet and see if his card is in it." The admittance nurse picked up her telephone and made a call and requested that all the personal items of the man in the emergency operating room be brought to her. The only items Marcus had had on him were his wallet, watch and a set of car keys, the ones to the rented SUV. She opened his wallet and found his insurance card and handed it to the nurse. After ten more minutes of answering the nurse and filling out forms, the admittance nurse led Sam to a waiting room and was told someone would come and get her as soon as her friend Marcus was out of emergency and she could visit with him. She pointed out a rest room where Sam could freshen up. When Sam came out of the rest room she returned to the admittance nurse's office and knocked on the door. Sam assumed that twenty minutes had passed and when the nurse asked if there was something else she could do for her. Sam told the nurse she wanted her to call the police. She had something that she wanted to say to them. It took more than five minutes before a young police officer met with her in the waiting room. When Sam related what had happened to her and Marcus and the men who had shot at them, the officer said he needed to talk to the sheriff and he excused himself and said he needed to return to his car. It wasn't long before the sheriff and two additional officers met with Sam in the waiting room. She quickly related to the sheriff what had happened and how she and Marcus got to the hospital. The sheriff wanted her to accompany them to the sheriff's office, but she was adamant about staying at the hospital. They were interested in the shooting and the men who had temporarily kidnapped her and Marcus. The sheriff let her know that he was upset that she hadn't called them sooner. She didn't mention the promise to Tony. She said, "I was too interested in getting Marcus in the hospital and too concerned about his well-being."

The event with the mountain lion came up and the sheriff accepted what she told him about the attack. As soon as she told them about the Winds Motel where they took her, the sheriff talked into his phone that someone from his office needed to check it out. The particulars about the money they had found were gone over for a second time and the fact that they hid it in their car, a blue Ford Taurus. It wasn't three minutes before the sheriff's phone rang and he took the call. When the call was finished, he reported that the shooters were gone and yes, there was a blue Ford Taurus there and the trunk had been broken into. When the police were finished with the questions they asked and she answered, they wanted to be able to reach Sam and wanted to know where she would be. "The only place I know in this town is the Twin Pines Motel, I'll be there or here in the hospital," she told the sheriff.

As soon as the police left, Sam asked a nurse if there was some place in the hospital where she could get something to eat, was told yes and was pointed toward a cafeteria. She took ten dollars from Marcus' wallet and headed toward it. It wasn't a cafeteria but a small café type restaurant that had a soup of the day, small salads, sandwiches, coffee and various other drinks, and deserts. A grill in the back room made a limited type of grilled sandwiches. After she had gotten something to eat she returned to the waiting area, sat in an armchair, closed her eyes and fell asleep. It was late afternoon when she was awakened by the admittance nurse. "He's out of danger and on the hospital's second floor in a private room, 204," she said. "The doctor cleaned the wounds and stitched them closed. His finger was not broken, only badly bitten. He is full of antibiotics and his fever has gone down. He will have to keep his arm in a sling for a while when he is released, most likely for at least a week to ten days. He will be in pain for a few days, but the doctor will prescribe some pain pills. You can see him, but he will be unconscious for a while. Doctor Lee said you brought him here just in time. Any longer the infection would have done permanent damaged to his heart and kidneys,"

"Thank you! Thank you!" Sam said to her.

Before she could say anything more the nurse pointed to her right and said, "There's the elevator."

Sam hurried out of the room, took the elevator to the second floor and found room 204. The door was open, and she could see Marcus on the hospital bed. She recognized a heart monitor, and he was getting an IV. She assumed fluids with more antibiotics, and she hoped a pain killer. She went to him and brushed his forehead and whispered, "I love you. I'm so happy you've come back to me." She kissed him on the cheek and went to the one chair in the room and sat down. "I'll wait right here until you wake up," she said to him.

Chapter 9

The next morning Sam was sitting, but asleep in the chair in the hospital room. Her clothes were dirty and there was dried blood on them, the same clothes she wore yesterday. On her lap was an open magazine. The only noise in the room were the beeps the heart monitoring machine made.

It was to the side of Marcus' bed and indicated that he was alive.

A slight knock on the door awakened Sam. Agent Corry Larson entered the room. She looked at Marcus and asked Sam, "How is he?"

Sam quickly was awake and answered the agent, "Doctor said he will be okay. He is sleeping now. He awoke earlier this morning and I talked to him, but he went back to sleep. We were lucky to get here when we did. Doctor Lee came by earlier to check on him and we talked a little. Told me the lion's mouth had some sort of very viral virus. Probably from rotten meat it had eaten. The bite transferred some of it to Marcus and it could have killed him. Spread through his body quickly and attacked some of his vital organs. Antibiotics have taken care of it."

"Glad to hear he'll recover. You've been here over a day now and you look beat," Agent Larson told Sam. "I'll take you back to your motel. You can use a hot shower, get some food and clean clothes. The local sheriff talked to me and told me what you said happened to you and to the money. Anything else you can add to what you told the police?"

"No," Sam said. "I think I told them everything."

"We went to their motel. I saw the blue Ford there, the trunk broken into. They were gone and so was the money," the agent told her. "The sheriff's crime scene investigation team is dusting the car for fingerprints. He will probably be able to find out who they were and will go after them."

All Sam could say was, "So they got the money."

"Sure seems that way," Ms. Larson replied. "Several weeks after the airplane crashed it began to turn cold and a skin of ice was on the lake. Never thought to look in the lake when we first searched. We will start searching the lake in a couple of days, maybe find the rest of it."

"You are assuming one of your treasury guards, Agent Beale, took it all and hid it. If he did, Marcus and I should have found more," Sam said to her. "When he first talked to you, Marcus told me that you said there were a total of fifteen cases. If they were hidden in the lake, surely we would have found more than one."

"Maybe yes, maybe no. Seems like he took it. Points more and more in that direction. He would have had to make several trips from the plane and would have gone close to the same spot on the lake. All he would have needed to do was to follow his footprints in the snow. Didn't matter to Beale where he hid them," Agent Larson said. "If, like you said, the case was filled with water, the suitcases could have broken free from the bottom and move around in the lake but not come to the surface. If they did surface could have been blown across the lake and be on the opposite side, maybe sunk there. After a year or so he could go back and look, sure he would be able to find at least one of them," she continued. "Like I said, we will find the cases."

Sam replied, "If they are in the lake." As an afterthought, Sam asked, "And Turner?"

"He's disappeared too," Agent Larson said. "First look appears that he was the one in on it with the guys who shot at you. No other way they could have found out about the money so quickly. He had to have been the one to tell them where you were, why they got to your motel so quickly."

Sam was a little saddened to hear about Agent Turner and she told Agent Larson, "Sorry to hear about him. He seemed so nice and sincere when he found us."

"Money does funny things to people. Can quickly make them dishonest. We won't ever stop looking for him nor the money." Agent Larson paused for a moment and said convincingly, "Quite a coincidence that his phone was dead and soon after he left, you said the guy called Joey, showed up. It's plausible that the two were traveling in different directions on the same road."

"If he was in it with them, why didn't he tell them where we hid the money?" Sam asked. "I had to tell them it was in our car."

"When we catch them, I'll ask him, and we will catch them," was the agent's answer. "Might be he thought that he could get it, keep it all for himself. For sure he didn't get to your car or your keys before they did, or they wouldn't have had to hot wire the car to start it and break into the trunk."

It was four days later and Sam was driving their rented Taurus. Marcus was released from the hospital that morning and they returned to their old motel room, packed up all their stuff and began the drive to Denver. They talked briefly about running into the three men who had been after them when they reached Denver. Agent Larson told them that fingerprints at the Winds Motel came back positive on two of them. One was Anthony Ricci and a Joseph Garza. Both are low level thugs for an organized crime boss, Gino Garza in Denver. They thought it very unlikely that they would ever see any of the gangsters again. She was driving and said to Marcus, "No matter what we do in the future or where we go, nothing will ever top this. How do you like that your arm is in a sling?"

He smiled and looked at her, "Only for about a week. You are going to have to wait on me hand and foot. Doc said I shouldn't stress it. Would be just like we were married."

"Huh!' she said. "If I wasn't on your hurt side, I'd punch you on the shoulder!"

"And you didn't want to go camping in the mountains," he continued.

"Who knew?" she said. "If you get tired. Let me know and we will stop, just say so."

"No, I'm okay Sam. We will stop at Glenwood Springs and check it out, can't be more than an hour from here. Nurse in the hospital talked it up and said we should see it. Said it's a touristy place but there's some good restaurants there. We can have a good meal before we get to Denver and then home."

"Did we buy auto insurance when we rented the car?' she wanted to know. When Marcus didn't immediately answer, she said, "Guess we will have to pay for the trunk lock."

"It's not that big of a deal. If we must pay for it, we will," he replied.

"Sorry about the money Marcus. You were more important to me, even if I have to wait on you hand and foot," she said to him.

That evening after they reached Glenwood Springs and checked into a motel, they walked into the town area and stopped at a restaurant that bragged about its old west food. The interior had a western feel. The floor, where it could be seen, was wooden and covered with peanut shells that were scattered all over it. On the walls was a considerable number of pictures of the old west, cowboys, miners, settlers, wagon trains and interspersed with the photographs were a number of western items, saddles, boots, spurs, coils of rope and guns. Then there were the mining items, picks and shovels, head lamps, canteens, boots, and gold pans. To lend a little more authenticity to it, in the gold pans were several what Marcus thought were spray painted gold rocks. The weapons could have been real, but Marcus believed that the ones he could see were so rusted to render them unusable or were non-firing replicas. The seats at the bar were saddles. When they were shown to their booth, the hostess handed them menus and said that Michelle would be their waitress. She would be with them in a moment. Michelle showed up dressed in western wear and wearing cowboy boots, a western style dress, wore a bandanna around her neck, a western style hat and she had two holsters with what looked like cap guns. She sat a bag of peanuts in the shell on the table. She introduced herself and told them she would be their waitress. "Just drop the shells on the floor," she said to them. "Can I get you something to drink?

The first thing that Marcus asked was, "Peanuts were a western food staple?"

"No sir, peanuts weren't. But to create the western feel we use peanuts and their shells to litter the floor. A real western bar or restaurant would have had sawdust on the floor, but it is too dusty, so peanut shells which are not quite as dusty are used. One big drawback of the shells is that they are noisy when you step on them."

Sam ordered an iced tea and Marcus just water. After she brought them their drinks they both ordered the 'chuck wagon special' which was not more than a house salad, steak, baked potato, beans, and another vegetable of the day, that happened to be steamed broccoli, and a desert. "The place has a lot of character," Sam said looking around.

"Don't know how much of this stuff is the real thing, or just hype to fool us and other tourists," Marcus replied.

Sam continued to look around at the items on the walls and said, "It doesn't matter. It looks real and gives the place character."

"Yeah," replied Marcus. "Look at that wooden saddle for mules."

She looked to where he was pointing and asked, "How do you know that?"

He just smiled at her and said, "I just do. I'm quite knowledgeable."

Their conversation about the interior of the restaurant was interrupted when their waitress brought them their food. "Which of you didn't want sour cream or butter on their potato?" she asked.

"That's hers," he told the waitress.

When she asked if she could get them anything else, Sam pointed at the wooden saddle and asked, "Michelle, is that wooden looking saddle for mules?"

"Oh no. It can be, I guess. It's a pack saddle for mules or horses. See all of the holes in it and the rings?" she said. "That is so that whatever a miner wanted to pack into his claim he would have somewhere or something to tie it off to."

"Thank you very much for that information Michelle. I believe that will be all," and Sam began to cut into her steak as the waitress walked away. She watched out of the corner of her eye as Marcus tried to hold his fork in his left hand, despite the sling, and cut the meat with his right. He struggled. Finally, she asked, "Well Mr. knowledgeable man, would you like some help?"

Without looking up he replied, "My mistake. Saw one on the prospector's mule, belonged to that old miner. Assumed he put it on his mule and rode."

They finished dinner and arm in arm headed back to their motel. They were walking on the pedestrian bridge that crossed I-70. Cars went zooming under them. When they reached the hot springs pool, they could look down on it for the second time and stopped and saw people swimming. "Tell you the truth Sam. I'm not very impressed. Looks just like another pool to me with a lot more people swimming now than when we saw it walking to the restaurant."

"Maybe it has something medicinal in the water. You want to go in? Maybe heal your neck and arm faster. I'll buy a swimsuit," she said to him.

He didn't have to think about the offer very long when he said, "I don't think so. Don't wish to get the bandages wet. I've had enough of water to last a lifetime."

"Anyone asks, we can say we at least saw it," she said.

"Maybe tomorrow we can drive to Aspen and see what all the hoopla is about it," Marcus said.

"With no snow, probably just another town with condos," Sam told him. "We passed the exit when we drove to Twin Pines. But we will stop anyway and we can say we had been to Aspen. Just won't say when. Why don't we return to our motel and turn in?"

They continued walking until they saw an ice cream shop, stopped, and got two cones, sat at an outdoor table and ate them, got up and continued to their motel. At their room, they stopped and Sam took out of her purse their key card. Neither took notice to the man walking past them in the hallway. The door lock clicked, and she pushed down on the latch and at the same time started to push the door open, Marco rushed them and pushed them into their room. Both tripped as they stumbled and fell forward until they ended up on the bed. Marcus was able to put his good arm out to break his fall onto the bed. In the dimly lit room Marcus heard the door being closed behind them and the room lights came on. "Well, well. Look who just dropped in," said Tony. He was sitting in an easy chair in a corner of the room and turned on the lamp on the bed table at his side. "Nice to see you again." At the room's table sat Joey and Benny. Joey turned on the lamp on the table. They got up and Tony said, "Keep them covered." Both Joey and Benny took out their guns and aimed them at Sam and Marcus. Marco, after he pushed them into the room, stood in front of the room's door. "Both of you, sit!" commanded Tony.

The first words that came out of Sam's mouth were, "How'd you get in here!?"

Tony replied, "Take a guess."

"What do you want," she asked next.

"I thought we were playing straight with each other lady. I know we got off to a bad start, but we had a deal," Tony said.

"Where's the money?" asked Joey.

All that Sam could say was, "I told you."

"It wasn't there. I'll make you talk bitch," and Joey took a step toward her.

"Joey, shut up and be quiet!" Tony forcefully said. He looked at Sam and said, "Well, tell us about it!"

Sam answered, "I told you the truth. We put the money in the trunk of our car."

"It wasn't there!" Tony said.

Sam quickly said, "I told you that Treasury Agent Jeffrey Turner found us first. I told him all about it. I told you to hurry and get us to the hospital if you wanted to beat him to the money."

Marcus who was listening to their conversation said, "He apparently beat you to it."

"Yeah! Well, someone we know in the sheriff's department said the money hasn't been recovered," Tony responded.

"The treasury agents and the sheriff believe that Turner was with you because he has disappeared too," Marcus said.

"This is a bull shit story! We know you have it, and we want it! Where is it! Where'd you put it!?" Joey demanded.

"Shut up Joey!" Tony said. "I'm not going to tell you again!" He turned his attention back to the two sitting at the table. "What makes you think the agent was with us?"

"It makes sense, all of you disappeared at the same time and the money is gone." Sam replied. "You and he were the only ones who knew about it and now it's gone. One or the other of you had to have taken it, that's why."

"Didn't the agent tell you about it?" Marcus asked.

"We don't know no treasury agent," Joey said.

"Then, how did you find out about the money and know to come to our motel room and know our names?" Marcus asked.

"Gino told us," Joey said.

"Who's he?" Sam asked.

"He's my uncle. Sent us to find out if you two located where the money was and could we get it," replied Joey.

Tony glared at Joey and said, "Shut up Joey! Don't make me tell you again!"

Marcus said to Tony, "Have your guy call his friend in the sheriff department and ask him if what we've told you is true."

Sam and Marcus could see that Tony was thinking about all that they had said. He finally said, "Shut them up in the bathroom Joey."

"I don't believe them," Joey said. "Let me make them talk. I can do it."

"I told you to shut up Joey. Do what I say!" the exasperated Tony said.

He hesitated with a hostile look on his face. Tony didn't say another word but only stared at Joey. It was quite clear that Tony was the boss of the three and expected his orders to be followed. When it was clear what Tony said, Joey roughly grabbed Marcus by the right arm and stood him up. Before he could grab Sam, she stood near Marcus and Joey with Benny, ushered them into the bathroom. Before Joey closed the door, he told them, "Not a peep outa ya."

After the door was closed Tony took out his cell phone and dialed Mr. Garza's number. He said to Benny, "Turn on the TV so they won't be able to hear what I say on the phone. When his boss answered, Tony reported on their progress, "They don't have it. We searched their car and room again. What do you want us to do?"

Tony heard Mr. Garza ask, "What's their story?"

Tony told him what the two had said, "Everyone believes that the treasury agent she told us about was with us and now we got the money and all of us got away. Said to have you check with your friend in the sheriff's office, to ask him."

"Sit tight. I'll get back to you," Tony heard, and he closed his cell.

"What did he say?" asked Benny who was standing near the bathroom door.

"Said to sit tight and we're gonna. He's gonna check and get back to us," Tony told his three companions and he looked directly at Joey, "and make sure that nephew of his listens to you!" Tony added.

In the bathroom, Sam asked, "What can we do?"

Marcus knew that they were in a tight spot and tried to ease Sam's worry, "Not much. We will have to wait and see what happens."

Sam was still concerned and asked, "Did he hurt your arm?"

Marcus answered her, "No."

They were quiet for a moment before Sam asked, "Do you think they will torture us like Joey wants?"

"I don't think so," replied Marcus. "We can't tell them what we don't know. I think that guy Tony believes us." He was quiet for a moment and said, "If we get the chance we'll make a break for it. Just be ready on a moment's notice."

Ten minutes had passed and the four of them were watching the TV when Tony's cell phone signaled that he was getting a call. He saw the read out who was calling him. He answered, "Yes sir Mr. Garza?" and the other three crowded around him so they could hear their boss.

They heard their boss say, "Seems that they were telling you the truth. The treasury agent and the money are missing. There are no missing or stolen cars in the area, so it's believed he left with the gunmen, the four of you."

Tony shook his head as if his boss could see him and said loud enough for the others near could hear, "So the sheriff and treasury think we were all in it together?"

He held his phone up so they could all hear Mr. Garza say, "Yes. If you were with that government man, you better come clean with me."

Tony said into the phone, "Mr. Garza, you know I've been loyal to you for years. I'd never do something like that."

Again, he held his phone up so they all could hear, "You better not have. I'd hunt you all down and kill you!"

"Yes sir. And what about these two?" Tony asked.

The four men who worked for Mr. Garza heard, "Leave them and get out of there."

"Will do," said Tony and he put his phone away.

"You all heard him," Tony said to the group "They are telling the truth, we have the money and the treasury guy is with us. If it's true, we shouldn't go back to Denver."

"What'll we do about those two?" Benny asked.

"Turn up the TV and we will sneak out. Make them think we are still here," he replied, "and head back to Denver."

Chapter 10

As uncomfortable as it was, Sam and Marcus put towels and the bathmat on the floor, sat on them, their backs against the wall. After a while they both fell asleep. A nearby air horn on a tractor awakened them as it entered the entrance ramp to I-70. He looked at his watch and Marcus felt Sam stir. He whispered, "Sam it's morning."

She replied, "I'm sore and my back hurts. Are they still out there?"

"I don't know but I hear noise," he said. He struggled to get up and went to the door and knocked. There was no response from the room. He knocked again, louder. When none of the four guys came to the door, he opened it a crack and looked into the room, saw no one and opened the door all the way. "No one is here Sam. They've gone."

She got up from the floor and walked to him. "They believed us," as she stretched and added, "I'm stiff as a board."

Marcus immediately said, "Let's clean up, pack our stuff and check out."

Putting their stuff in their suitcases she said, "Can we go have breakfast and then get out of here and head for Denver?"

"What about Aspen?" he asked.

It was easy to answer him, "Next stop, the Denver airport!"

They had breakfast, checked out and left. They saw what they thought was Aspen from the interstate and Marcus commented on the condos he could see. They were close to forty miles from Denver when Marcus' cell phone buzzed. When he answered it, he recognized Treasury Agent Corry Larson. Marcus turned his cell phone on speaker. The first thing she said to them was, "Thought you would like to know, we found Agent Turner."

"Already," Marcus replied. "Did he have the money?"

"No," she said into the phone. "He's dead. Found him in a small ravine off the side of an unused logging road about a mile from your motel."

"I'll be damned!" he said. "How did you find him?" Marcus asked.

They listened while the treasury agent said, "A couple hiking saw the body and called the police. It wasn't on the way to your shooter's motel, closer to Twin Pines. The road was not that well-traveled. He could have been there for weeks before someone found him. Our first thought was that he had a falling out with your shooters over the money or that he could identify them, and they killed him and dumped his body. It makes sense. We are not sure why they dumped his body near your motel or why they might have been returning. They already had the money, unless they forgot something and needed to retrieve it. We talked to the guests that were still at the motel and the check in counter-clerk, no one remembers seeing any of them go into the motel or a car that somebody got out of in the parking lot."

"I wouldn't have believed it. He seemed so nice and sincere," said Sam. "I liked him."

"How did Agent Turner die?" Marcus asked.

"Corner prelim said a hard blow to the back of the head," Ms. Larson told him. "Won't know for sure until he does an autopsy."

"Sounds like you have a lot of work ahead of you, and still no money," he said to her. "Like you said, could be that Turner had a falling out with his accomplice, or accomplices, assuming he had help."

They heard her say, "The sheriff is handling the murder and will be looking at the possibility of an accomplice. I'm sorry for Turner, I liked him too. I can't believe that he had anything to do with the missing money, but my concern is finding the money. Divers have arrived and we are setting up a base camp near the lake."

"I wish you luck," Marcus said.

Before he could cut her off, he heard her say, "Same to you. Thanks to both of you for what you've done. Have a safe flight home."

He repeated to Sam what they had heard. "Turner has been found and he'd been murdered. Apparently a falling out among thieves."

Sam replied, "Couldn't have been that. Those goons knew nothing about him or the money, or, they were the most believable liars I've ever met."

"So, you think someone else then?" he asked her.

He could see Sam shaking her head yes. "Had to be." Sam was quiet for a while before he asked, "Who?"

She replied. To his who and answered, "You're a detective, detect."

"What's that supposed to mean?" he asked, and she didn't say anything.

Chapter 11

It was early morning of the next day. Sam and Marcus were in one of the interview rooms of the Twin Pines Motel drinking coffee with Treasury Agent Cory Larson. "So where do you intend to start snooping around," Ms. Larson asked him.

"I'm thinking," he replied.

"Thinking about what?" Sam asked. He continued, "Here's what we know, Agent Turner didn't take the money. We know the gunmen didn't get it if what they said was true and we believed them."

"Video surveillance of the parking lot and the fingerprints found on your car belonged to two low level gangsters believed to work for a Denver mobster, Gino Garza. He must have been the one who Agent Turner told, if we believe the agent was mixed up in all of this. If he weren't with the gangsters, who else could have known about the money and taken it?" Ms. Larson asked.

To her question Marcus replied, "If we believe Turner was involved, he had to have a partner here in Colorado who he called and told, and it wasn't those goons. They had someone else tell them and you said they worked for a low-level gangster in Denver. It stands to reason someone told him and he sent two of his men to confront us."

"Those guys that took me to the hospital didn't know that we had money. They believed we knew where it was and maybe took some of it. I had to tell them, like I told Agent Turner, that we found and brought back over four million."

"That is what we need to find out. Who knew? Who did he tell? Did Turner have a partner? That's who we need to look for," Ms. Larson said.

The three of them were silent for a moment before Sam said, "Where do you propose we should start Marcus."

"That's easy," he replied, "at the beginning."

"Okay, where does the beginning start?" Sam wanted to know. "When we left San Francisco, when we got here, when we rented our camping gear and the ATV? When?"

He thought about it for a moment and said, "Let's trace our every step from the moment we found the money until the sheriff found our car broken into."

"Okay you've found the money. You said you scattered it around at your camp site to dry out a little. Is it possible someone saw you at the lake with the money?" was Ms. Larson's next question.

"I don't think so, if they saw us, we sure didn't see them, but I'll keep that as a possibility. If we were seen, why didn't that person tell the Denver gangster where we found the money? Begin looking for more in the lake? If we believe those four goons, they knew nothing about where we found the money," Marcus replied.

"Then we returned to the motel and anyone could have seen us. But all they would have seen were two campers returning on an ATV pulling a trailer behind it with our camping gear," Sam said.

"When you arrived at the motel, what did you do next," Ms. Larson asked.

"We unloaded our stuff," said Marcus. "Sam began sorting through it and I drove the ATV onto the trailer that came with an SUV we rented for a week."

Sam said, "I took some of our personal stuff into the motel, got my purse from security so that I could use my credit card, rented a room, got the Taurus car keys and took the stuff I had to our room, then back to the parking lot with Marcus."

"Why didn't you take your purse?" Ms. Larson asked.

"I didn't want to take it with me on our camping trip. Why would I need it? It had some money in it. Thought it safer in security storage," she replied.

I took my purse that had the car keys so that we could put some of what we were going to take back to California with us in the Taurus."

"What did you do with the money?" Ms. Larson asked.

"After I loaded the ATV, I got the keys from Sam and then I took the metal suitcase with the money in it to our car and locked it in the trunk," he said. "The blue Ford Taurus. She brought several items to the car and I locked them in the trunk also."

"Did anyone see you in the parking lot? Did you see anyone?" the agent asked.

"I suppose we could have been seen. For sure I don't remember seeing any one in the lot except for us," Sam said. "It was late morning and most of the motel's guests had left. The parking lot was almost empty. Few cars in the room's parking spaces."

Ms. Larson said that she would have earlier video parking lot footage checked to see if anyone had been in the area during the time the money was transferred to their car. She took out her cell phone and punched in some numbers. They heard her talk to Agent Irving Plank that he should get the surveillance tapes of the parking lot and see if anyone else was in the parking lot when Marcus and Sam returned from their camping. Then he should look forward to see who may have opened the trunk of their blue Taurus. When the call was over, she asked, "How about the receptionist?" Ms. Larson wanted to know. "Could he have seen you through the windows or door?"

"Don't think so," replied Marcus. "The SUV and our car where not in a place that anyone at the desk could see. Both were to the side and at would be the rear of the parking lot, couldn't be seen from the desk unless he walked to the entrance door, open it and looked to the side."

"According to the sheriff when his men talked to him, he had nothing that could help. He couldn't identify the shooters. Said he didn't pay them much attention when they entered the motel. They knew where your room was, never stopped at the desk and ask, but walked straight to the elevator. He assumed they were guests and was quite helpful to the local police when they showed up. Told the police where the two of you ran and which way you went and what the two of you looked like. He believed a third person joined them when they went into the woods looking for you and took the police to your room and pointed out the bullet holes.

"We know where the keys to the car came from and afterwards, where did you put them?" Ms. Larson asked.

"She gave them to me, and I returned them to her after I put the money in the trunk," Marcus said. "I saw her put them back in her purse."

Sam said, "You dropped me off after you drove me from the hospital and I got the motel receptionist get a bellboy to let me into our room, I had no card key. I cleaned up and I took the keys out when I was going to return to the hospital and realized that we longer had the car. I did tell Agent Turner about the keys and our car. Was there any evidence that the trunk lock was somehow picked?"

"Impossible to tell after the damage the shooters did when opening it." They thought about what had been said to this point when the Treasury Agent Larson asked, "Could someone in the motel have seen you?"

"Possibly," said Marcus. "But they would not have known that the suitcase held the money. As far as anyone would think, we were just unloading our camping stuff and what I may have placed in the trunk was something I didn't want to carry up to our room, maybe a suitcase with dirty camping clothes. Probably something that wasn't too important. But if we were seen, how did they get the keys from Sam's purse and then return them?"

"Then," Sam said, "we made two trips and carried everything up to our room. I did put some of the stuff we were not going to save, and the outfitter was not going to take back near the trash cans at the motel. I took a bath and Marcus called you from our room."

Then I called the desk and told them we would be staying a few extra days," Marcus added.

"Is it possible someone in the room next to yours overheard you on the telephone?" Ms. Larson asked.

"I guess that is a possibility, but I didn't talk that loud and I'm not sure they would have known what I was talking about," he replied. "And when I think back on it, our room was pretty soundproof. I never heard anything from the adjacent rooms, voices, the TV or radio."

"I think that we should consider it, but they would have had to be listening to us and what he was saying. Not a very good option," Sam said.

"I took a shower and we both got dressed and walked toward town, stopped at a diner close to the motel and got something to eat and went back to our room," Marcus said.

"Later that afternoon was when the two gangsters who said they were government agents sent by Washington showed up. When Marcus asked for some ID, that's when all hell broke loose. You pretty much know the rest."

"Did you talk to anyone when you went out?" the agent asked.

"Except to order from the waitress, no one," he said.

The two thought about what they had said and could add nothing more. Ms. Larson said, "Nothing stands out or is suspicious. You must be missing something. Did you talk about what you had found when you were eating? Maybe someone nearby overheard you?"

They were quiet for a moment when Sam spoke, "No. We talked about what we were going to do when we got back to San Francisco. That was it. Not a word about what we had found. I can't remember anything else."

"I believe the money was taken before the trunk was broken into," Ms. Larson said.

Marcus said, "A good car thief could have easily opened the trunk without a key."

"That brings us back to Agent Turner. He could easily have called someone in Denver, the boss of those goons. They knew to identify themselves as treasury agents," Ms. Larson said.

"And they knew about the money," he replied.

"No," said Sam.

"No what?" asked agent Larson.

Sam was quick to respond, "They said they were government agents, nothing was mentioned about treasury. If Turner told them, I'm sure they would have known he was with the treasury department. They didn't ask where the money was. They wanted to know if we found it, maybe took some. They were more interested in wanting to know where we found it."

"Maybe he called Gino Garza, Garza then called his goons. To be sure, Garza called a second party, and that fact was lost or overlooked," Ms. Larson replied. "Makes sense that that person then killed Agent Turner, in order to keep all the money for himself, he killed Turner. I'll be looking into his past, his friends, did he gamble, maybe do drugs."

"That scenario overlooks one thing," said Marcus. "The guys who showed up at our room, according to our conversation with them, knew nothing about Turner nor did their boss."

"Let's assume that Tuner may have told two people, Garza and a second person in the area about the money. It doesn't make much sense, but your original theory about him could hold water," Marcus said.

"I will return to Denver and follow up with Garza, why we know he was involved. How did he know to send some of his men here to question the two of you? How did he know? Who told him about the money? If it was someone in my office, I want to know who," Ms. Larson said. "I'll have the sheriff check if anyone is missing in the area or suddenly is spending a lot of money. I will be returning tomorrow morning to our base camp out at the lake. I'll check with Agent Plank and find out if anything showed up on the tapes. If either of you think of anything else call me or contact the sheriff's office. I won't be back for a couple of days, but I'll check with you before I leave," Ms. Larson said to them and she left.

That evening Treasury Agent Larson was again talking to Marcus and Sam. "The tapes didn't show much. They were eight-hour tapes with a combination of four camera shots. After two weeks, they would be recorded over. It was up to the receptionists to change them out every eight hours. Two different views of the parking lot, one including your car the second one the motel entrance. There was no coverage of you placing the suitcase in your car, a third one covered the pool area and one of the interior reception area. Each was a five second view before it switched to another camera. There was a glitz with the tape machine because there were several times when it was all snow. First for a few seconds then they lasted for close to a minute, sometimes starting or stopping in the middle of a scene. The glitzes started before your return and then off and on until well after you ran into the woods and the police showed up. The next several days the glitzes continued but showed nothing up until the time when we arrived. One showed one of Garza's men steal your car and drive off with it. When this problem was pointed out to the motel manager, she was going to replace the machine."

"And what about Garza?" Marcus asked.

"Nothing," replied the treasury agent.

"Questioned him about what happened and he denied everything and I got nowhere. If some of the men who allegedly work for him were involved, it was upon them. He did not order it. Any sort of involvement I'd have to talk to them. Needless to say, none of them were available to question."

The next morning, they slept in and by the time they showered and dressed it was past one o'clock in the afternoon. When they finally were ready, Sam said, "Let's walk to that diner and get something to eat." Marcus agreed it was a good idea and she added, "Get your cell from the charger so that you can call your chief. Tell him you may be a few days late getting back."

"I'm already two days past my vacation time," he told her.

"Say you are not recovering as quickly from the lion bite as you and your doctor hoped. He thinks you should stay for a couple of more days for him to monitor you," she said. "Maybe you will have to take an extra week of vacation, or sick leave."

Marcus agreed with her, left their table, and went to an empty area of the diner. Sam could see him talking on his cell phone. He told her he called and felt a little bad about lying to his boss. They ate at the diner and returned to their motel room. Sam said it was going to be a nice day and she was going to go out to the pool area and read and get some sun. Marcus wanted to drive to the sheriff's office and talk to him and wanted to know if she wanted to go with him. When she said no, she asked, "You sure you will be able to drive with one arm, not use your left arm?"

"My shoulder feels better, I can manage. I've taken off the sling. Should I leave the cell or take it with me?" Marcus asked.

At the door with a magazine under her arm she answered him, "Keep it with you. I won't need to make a call and if I do, I'll use the phone in our room."

He was heading toward the door following her and asked her if she had her card key to the room. When she said yes, he pulled his wallet from his front pocket and checked to make sure he had his. He replaced it to his normal back left pocket. She went to the motel's pool; he went to their car. He started the car and began to back out of his spot when he stopped. A look of surprise was on his face. He slapped the steering wheel and pulled back into his spot. He got out of his car and headed for the motel entrance, opened the door and walked straight to the check-in desk. He asked the woman there, "If I need to make a long-distance phone call from my room and ask you to give me an outside line, what would you do?"

She gave him a big smile and said, "I would take your room number, type it into our switch board monitor and connect you and you could make your call. Shall I do it for you sir?"

"No," he said. "Could you listen in on my conversation?"

She quickly answered him, "No. All I can do is give you an outside line. There is no way for me to overhear you. The most I would be able to do is see the read out on our main switch board monitor, the number you called. It would tell me how long you talked and how much to bill your room. Most are only a standard amount. When we get the phone bill at the end of the month I also would know the city with that number."

Satisfied with her answer he asked, "What is the name of the check-in guy?"

"Which one sir, we have two," was her response.

Marcus thought back and said, "He was tall and thin. Looked like he would always need a shave."

That was all that she needed to hear when she said, "Oh. You mean Dave Winters, the hunter."

"Is he around?"

"No."

"What does that mean, the hunter?" he asked her.

"He's not around. Must really be ill, called in sick couple of days after the shooting we had here, and I haven't seen him since. Not like him. I've been filling in for him, working two shifts. He works seven in the morning till three. Not like him to miss work. We refer to him as the hunter because he is always shooting some poor defenseless animal and offering it to people that work here at the motel," she answered.

"Where does he live, I need to talk to him," Marcus told her.

She hesitated and finally said, "I don't know if I'm allowed to tell you."

"You know I'm with the treasury people staying here," and he reached around behind him and struggled. He eventually was able to fish out his wallet. He flipped it open to reveal his police badge.

She didn't study it or see that it was a San Francisco police badge. All she did was basically repeat what she had told him, "Still, we are not supposed to give out personal information."

Marcus persisted, "Doesn't that apply only to guests? I can always look up his address in the telephone book now that I know his name."

He saw her hesitate and could see her thinking about what he had just said and so he pressed on. "And you can save me some time by telling me how to get to his place."

"Well, I guess it won't hurt," she said. "I don't know his address, our manager does. He lives on Renegade Road. The afternoon receptionist, Ashley, pointed it out to me once. The last, yellow greenish, single story house on your right. His house is on the edge of a bunch of pine trees. When Renegade Road splits into a Y, you've gone too far."

"Okay," said Marcus. "Tell me how I find Renegade Road."

"Go back into town. The first street past the post office is Birch, turn left and in a mile or so, Renegade crosses it, turn right. His house is about another mile."

Marcus thanked her and headed out to the pool. He saw Sam sitting under an umbrella and walked to her. She looked up at him and said, "That was quick."

He sat down beside her and said, "We did not tell Agent Larson everything. We left something out."

"Which was?" she asked.

Marcus said, "Our cell was dead when I tried to call Washington. I had to use the motel phone and ask the desk clerk for help me get an outside line."

"Yes, and what does that have to do with anything? Could the clerk listen in on your conversation," she wanted to know. "Was he seen on the video tapes taking the money?"

"No to both Sam. But he has not been seen for a while. Called in and said he was sick. It might be a long shot but is it possible that he is involved?" asked Marcus.

"How, if he couldn't hear what you talked about?" she responded

"I don't know. Ms. Larson dismissed him, but he is the one person we never talked about," he replied. "It's already after three. Think about it. Maybe he was looking out and saw what we did when we returned with the ATV. After we have dinner, what say we take a ride out to his place and talk to him?"

Chapter 12

It was after six o'clock and Sam was driving. Marcus gave her the instructions he was given, and she just turned left onto Birch street. When she had driven two miles she said, "The girl may have told you a mile or so, and it is so. We've already gone three miles. Maybe we passed it and didn't notice it." She no sooner said that when they saw a sign on the side of the road that indicated they were coming to Renegade Road. Sam slowed down and stopped at the stop sign and then pulled out and turned right. I hope that this is not several miles like the girl told you.

Marcus was about to answer her when he spotted the house. It needed to be painted and the yard was littered with various pieces of junk in knee high weeds and grass. As the receptionist at the motel said, it was a sickly yellow house that sat near a shrub pine tree forest that stretched as far as Marcus could see. Occasionally a full-grown pine tree or a white birch tree could be seen. Years ago, the area had been clear cut. He couldn't see very deep into the trees because smaller pine trees sprouted everywhere between the larger pines that had been over-looked. It appeared as a wall. On the opposite side of the road were full grown pine trees. To the side of the house was a garage, no door or if there was one it was up, and the garage was leaning to one side. In it was a mud-spattered pickup. Extending beyond the house at its rear he could see a stack of cut firewood about six feet high. The sun was descending behind the mountains to the west when Marcus said, "That's his house. Pull in."

Sam pulled into the driveway. Forty yards from the house she parked to one side and turned off the engine. Without looking at him she asked, "What do you intend to do detective?"

Marcus said, "You stay in the car. If I don't come out in ten minutes, call the sheriff. I'll leave my cell here in the car for you." Sam took the cell and threw it into her purse.

Marcus got out of the car and started up the driveway and saw an overgrown stone walkway that led from the driveway to the front door. He began to walk to the house. Before he reached the two steps up to the concrete pad that served as a porch and the door of the house, he could hear a dog barking. The deep sounds of the barks made him believe that it was a big dog. He looked for a doorbell, couldn't find one, so he knocked. In a moment, the door opened a crack, the barking was louder, and he could see the head of a large dog. The dog appeared to be being held and then pulled back. He could hear a voice telling the dog to get down. The door opened further and Marcus saw the man who was at the check-in counter when he registered at the motel, but he asked if he was Mr. Winters. The man shook his head yes and Marcus wanted to know if he could come in. He heard, "I'll hold the dog down, yes, come in." Marcus tentatively entered the house.

When Marcus was in the house he saw it was the dining room of what he believed was a male dominated house. The entire dining room was a man's cave. There was a dining table and above it, a chandelier. Four chairs were at the table. There were two stuffed deer heads mounted on the pine wall above a buffet. There were other stuffed animals and birds scattered about the room, some were hanging on the walls and others were in a pose. There was a large, framed photo of Dave holding up the head of a large dead elk. He was somewhat impressed when he saw the large male turkey with its tail spread out in a fan just to the side of an old cabinet style TV. Where the walls were not decorated with a stuffed animal or bird, there were pictures of hunting dogs, hunters, and various animals. The room had a fireplace and there was a pile of split pieces of wood to one side. Above the fireplace was a gun rack with four long guns of different types. There were two doorways leading out of the room. One he could see went to the kitchen the other he assumed to the interior rooms.

Dave Winters yelled in a commanding voice, "Tripper, get down! Get over here and sit!" The dog followed his command and the dog stared at Marcus. "What can I do for you?" Dave asked.

As soon as he was in the dining room, Marcus asked, "Remember me? The day of the motel shooting?"

Dave Winters looked at him and said, "Vaguely. You were the one the men shooting was after. I guess they didn't get you."

"No, they didn't," Marcus answered.

"Your name is Marc something, right?" Dave said. Then with his arm he indicated that Marcus should sit at one of the dining table chairs. "What was that all about anyway?"

"Name's Marcus," the detective replied. "They thought I had something that they wanted."

Dave Winters pulled out a chair opposite Marcus at the table and sat. "So, what can I do for you Marcus?" he asked.

"I want to ask you some questions about that day. Your name's Dave, right?" Marcus asked him.

Dave immediately said, "Forgive me. I'm a poor host. I should know better. Let me get you a drink. I have sodas, coffee and bottled water."

"Nothing, I'm fine," Marcus said.

"Well," Dave said as he was getting up, "I'm going to get myself a Coke. You sure you don't want anything?" Marcus just shook his head no when Dave said he'd be right back. He turned and walked into the kitchen and disappeared around the corner.

When Dave left, Tripper got up and walked over close to Marcus and sat. He could see that the dog was part German Shepard and part, he believed, Rottweiler or the other way around. The way the dog looked at him, Marcus thought that the dog looked dangerous. He put his hand out, palm down for the dog to lick and smell when he heard a low, deep growl. He thought better of it and slowly pulled his hand back. He asked in a loud voice, "Is this dog friendly?"

Marcus heard Dave say as he was coming from the kitchen, not holding a Coke, but a rifle and it was pointed at Marcus. "Unless I sic him on you, and then you'll be sorry."

"Whoa! Whoa! What's the rifle for?" Marcus almost shouted.

"Both hands, flat on the table, palms down. Try anything funny and Tripper will tear you apart. I was wondering how long it would be before someone asked additional questions about the shooting and the fact that the parking lot cameras didn't show what was needed, that showed you putting a metal suitcase in the trunk of your car. I checked the video the next day after the shooting. Not even that gangster Garza or his men suspected. When the treasury agent asked to show them the tape, I pulled up the ones for that day. It as well as the next day showed no image but occasionally, snow until it showed you running into the trees. I guess it cleared up. No one asked for earlier ones. If they would have, I had gone back and taped nothing so that they showed snow. A problem with the machine. I guess today is the day." Keeping the rifle aimed at Marcus, Dave told the dog to watch him. The dog got up, took half a step closer to Marcus and growled, baring its teeth.

Marcus was sure that the dog understood what its master had said. "People know that I came here," he told Dave.

"Yeah, who?" He threw a partial roll of duct tape on the table toward Marcus. "Tape your legs to the legs of your chair. Don't even think of trying anything. This .300 Savage will make a big hole in you."

Marcus was having trouble tearing the tape after he wrapped one leg. Dave threaten to shoot him where he sat and didn't want to hear any story about a mountain lion biting him on his left shoulder. Doubling his effort Marcus was able to tear the tape and to tape his other leg. "Now tape your right wrist to the chair's arm." He struggled but could wrap the roll around the chair's arm and his wrist several times. He definitely was sure he would not be able to tear the tape with his left hand. Dave had a solution. He walked around the table to where Marcus was, took out of its sheath on his belt, a large hunting knife, again warned his dog to be alert, and cut the tape. He replaced the knife to its sheath and had Marcus put his left wrist on the arm of his chair and with one hand Dave quickly taped his wrist down.

"You're not going to be able to get away with this. I'll be missed, questions will be asked," Marcus said. "The sheriff is already searching for the murderer of the treasury agent. Only a matter of time till he gets around to you."

"Heard it on the news. Never thought that the agent would have been found so soon on that side road. Thought I'd go back and bury him some night. Went out to get firewood from my truck, had parked it beside your car. Caught me closing your trunk and I had your car keys. A quick blow to the back of his head with a piece of firewood. Loaded him in the bed of my truck. Looked around and saw no one. No one saw me. Covered him and the suitcase with a tarp and went back inside. Put the keys back in her purse. I was questioned. Told the sheriff's deputy I didn't see a thing; I was on duty and had to stay behind the reservation counter. Knew that I would most likely be questioned again and was sure that the sheriff would want to look at the tapes covering the parking lot. Began to pull all the tapes and look at them. I decided to take the tape that showed me doing what I had done. Thought that it would be checked and missed if it disappeared. Only person that could have removed it was a motel employee. Most likely me. That was when I decided to make it look like the tape machine messed up, didn't record some of the time on your tape. Went back almost to the beginning, well before you loaded the money in your car so it wouldn't look too suspicious. Learn from your mistakes. Anybody can ask. You were never here. I'll throw your body into one of the abandoned mine shafts around here, so deep you will never be found," Dave replied.

"Want to know about the rest of the money?" Marcus asked.

"No. Shut up. Get greedy, you get caught. Four million plus is plenty enough for me," was Dave's response. "If you would have known you would have told those treasury people. Hear they are getting ready to search the lake." After a moment he heard a noise, "What was that?" Dave asked and walked to a window and looked out. The sound he had heard was a car door slamming shut. "I see you brought your girlfriend along. Well, I'll take care of her too."

Chapter 13

Sam waited in the car when she saw Marcus go into the house. After three minutes, from around the garage two balls of fur, puppies, came running out and went to the car. They began yapping. Sam left her purse on the car's seat and got out of the car. She knelt on the ground and as soon as she did the two puppies were running around her and jumping across her legs. She reached down and patted the two which only got them more excited as they yipped and yapped wanting more attention and patting.

At the same time, Dave opened the door and called to her, "Lady! Come in! He needs help! His arm is bleeding! Hurry!"

Sam stood up, hurried around the car, and started for the house. When she did, she heard Marcus yell, "Run Sam! Run! He's the one! Get help!"

At the yells from Marcus in the house, she turned and ran toward the car. When she did, Dave brought the rifle up and fired a shot at her. She was too far from the car and would be in the wide open, so she veered off to her left and entered the scrub pine forest as another shot was fired at her.

Back at the house Dave said, "Get her Tripper," and he urged the dog out the door. He watched for a second as the dog entered the trees where the woman had run. He turned and looked at Marcus, "Another mistake, should have taped your mouth. No matter. Tripper will catch her and most likely will not be a pretty sight. We'll just wait until he returns."

"There's a lot of money out there, we could share it. Each of us could go our separate way." There was no response from Dave. But Marcus continued, "Aren't you listening? Aren't you interested?"

Dave Winters did not answer Marcus. He sat there in silence. Marcus didn't know how long the dog had been searching for Sam, but it seemed to him it was a long time. He heard Dave say, "Should have seen the bear that Tripper attacked two years ago. Not much left of it when he got finished."

Marcus saw through the window that it was getting dark. The room was also getting dark and Dave made no attempt to turn on any lights. Now that the light in the room made it difficult to see, Marcus struggled. He strained at the tape on his right wrist but was unable to make the slightest space for his wrist to move. Several layers of duct tape were going to be difficult to tear. He tried to loosen his left arm with the same results, and it hurt his shoulder. His concentration on loosening his wrists from the chair was broken when he heard scratching from the kitchen. Dave got up and walked to the kitchen with his rifle and turned on the kitchen light and disappeared around the corner. Marcus tried harder to loosen his wrist or tear the tape as soon as his captor left. Light from the kitchen spilled into the dining room and he could hear a door in the kitchen being opened and closed, then Dave say, "Her blood. Good boy." There was a moment of silence and then Marcus heard, "My God, it's not hers! What has happened to your eye! Stay! I'll kill the bitch! I'll get you to the vet! Hold on." Marcus could hear the door open and be closed again. He struggled more to loosen his wrists. He bent his head down and was able to get his teeth under the tape on his right wrist. He chewed on the tape and felt a small tear start. He continued to chew and felt the tear get bigger, but he could not loosen it enough to free his wrist.

Outside Dave Winters was in the scrub pines. He shouted, "I know you are out here! I'm gonna' find you! Make it easy on yourself." There was no response so he continued, "All you need to do is give me a head start and the two of you will be free to go. I'll even give you half of the money. You hear, half!" He stopped and listened. He heard nothing and said, "I'm not mad about my dog. He's going to be okay. I'll take him to the vet."

Samantha could hear him and continued to move slowly away from where she believed him to be. Pine tree boughs brushed across her face and an occasional branch scratched her face and arms. She began to use the tree branch she was using as a cane to feel in front of her to avoid what she could not see. Sam could not determine how close he was. After a few steps, she stopped and listened, heard nothing, and continued to walk. It was quiet walking among the small pine trees because of the pine needles on the ground. It was getting darker outside and the small pine trees seemed to make it darker. To the east, she could see a sliver of moon just clearing the mountains. It was going to be a dark night. When she thought she would be able to get away, Samantha stepped on a dead pine branch and it broke with a loud snap. She swore to herself under her breath. She had been concentrating on the small trees in front of her, not the ground. The breaking dead branch sounded like a gunshot to her in the quiet pines. She was sure that Dave heard it and would be headed in her direction. She kept on moving, but slowly and carefully.

In the dining room Marcus continued to struggle with the tape. The tear seemed to get larger. He stopped struggling when he heard the dog's toenails clicking on the floor as the dog walked into the dining room from the kitchen. From the light coming into the dining room from the kitchen, he could see blood running from its eye onto its muzzle as it approached him. It let out a low growl. Its mouth and its teeth showed telltale signs of blood. Not sure what the dog would do if he continued to struggle, he said in a low soft voice, "Easy boy, easy." The dog didn't seem to pay him any mind, so he continued talking to it. "That's a good dog. Lie down." The dog didn't seem to pay any attention to Marcus. It walked to one side so that it was out of the direct light coming through the kitchen doorway and laid down. It began to lick its chin and upper lip as far as its tongue would reach. "Your attack can't be as bad as the lion's," he whispered to the dog as he continued to twist his right wrist left and then right. Each twist put strain on the tape. He couldn't get his jaws any further under the tape to tear more. In a last desperate attempt, he firmly grasped the end of the chair's arm and tried to stand up. He hoped that the leverage of his lower arm would either tear the tape the rest of the way or he was going to break his wrist trying. It hurt but he continued applying pressure and the tape tore. He pulled his arm away from the chair's arm and quickly began to unwrap his left wrist. All the time he kept an eye on the dog. His left wrist was now untaped and he slowly bent down and started to remove the tape from his legs. When he was free, he slowly stood up and began to move away from the chair. The ambient light from the kitchen was enough for him to see and he saw the dog watch him, but the dog did nothing. He went to the gun rack above the fireplace, checked and found all the guns were unloaded. A quick look showed him there were no shells anywhere to be found. He returned to the other side of the table, keeping it between him and the dog. He was about to go into the kitchen when he heard the dog growl. He stopped and inched his way to the kitchen doorway. Tripper continued his low growl but did not make any sort of move toward Marcus. At the doorway, he looked at the dog and saw that it was busy licking its muzzle, so he walked into the kitchen expecting at any moment the dog to lunge at him.

In the kitchen, he began to look for anything he could use as a weapon. He picked up and then rejected a small frying pan. From the sink, he grabbed a small paring knife and then also rejected it. Grabbing a drawer handle he opened the silverware drawer. He picked out a butcher knife and headed for the door and was soon outside.

Outside Samantha had neared the edge of the scrub pine trees and could see their car. Not sure where he might be, she looked back over her shoulder and continued to move until she was opposite their car. She burst out of the pine scrubs and made a dash for it. She reached the car, grabbed the handle, and opened the door and jumped in. She reached for the keys to start the car and they were not in the ignition where she had left them. From behind her Dave said, "Looking for these?" and he held up the car keys.

Terrified Samantha reacted by scooting across the seat to the passenger side of the car. She grabbed hold of the handle and was about to open the door and get out when Dave raised his rifle and shot out the passenger side window. She stopped, her ears ringing from the noise the rifle made. The ringing in her ears didn't prevent her from hearing him say, "Get out! Let's go you bitch!" and he grabbed her by the ankle and pulled her across the seat toward him. Once outside the car she stood up and Dave Winters marched her to his front door. He indicated the doorknob and she opened it. He pushed her in.

Chapter 14

When he was outside, Marcus started to head for the scrub pine forest. He had not gone more than several feet into it when he heard Dave speak to Sam. He saw Dave at the car and heard the shot. He believed Dave had shot her. But then he could see the car's interior light shine on Sam and he watched as he saw Dave pull her out of the car and march her up the driveway and follow the stone walkway to the front door. He watched as Sam opened the door and he then pushed her in and followed. After the door closed Marcus could see light come through the dining room window.

In the dining room Dave angrily spit out, "Fuck! Where'd he go!? God-damn it!" He looked at the dog, "Why didn't you stop him!?" He pulled out a chair from the table and in the same breath said, "Sit bitch!" He taped Samantha to the chairs arms the same way Marcus had been taped. When he had finished, he said, "Now your mouth. Learn from your mistakes" as he wrapped a strip of duct tape over her mouth. He took a step toward the dog, pointed to the woman taped to the chair and said to the dog, "Watch her Tripper." The dog stood up and took a step closer to Samantha. It laid down. Looked at her and a low growl could be heard.

Dave turned the chandelier lights in the dining room out and went to the kitchen. He opened one of the drawers and began moving items around in it. He removed a flashlight. He turned the kitchen lights out and the flashlight on. He swept it quickly around the kitchen and through the doorway to the dining room and he picked out Tripper and then moved the light to Samantha. Again, he talked to the dog, "Watch her!" he commanded. He shined the light on the kitchen door, opened it and went outside. Marcus could see him sweep the beam of the flashlight over the scrub pines, stop and then the light could be seen as Dave enter the trees.

A moment passed before he opened the front door and Marcus looked into the room. He couldn't see anything, and he whispered, "Sam, are you in here?" There wasn't an answer, but he could hear her muffled sound of, "Mmmmm." He looked to the sound and in the dark room could see her shape at the table. "I see you," he whispered. "I'm coming. I'll have you free in a second." Marcus moved as quickly as he could in the dark room. When he thought he was in arm's length from her he heard the definite low growl of the dog. He stopped for a second and in a soft and quiet voice he told the dog to be a good boy and lie down. Marcus couldn't see the dog, what it might be doing but he held the butcher knife in a defensive posture. If the dog attacked him, he would stab it. He could hear the dog growl again, but he decided to chance it and took the last steps to where he could see the basic shape of Sam silhouetted against the little bit of moon light that came through the kitchen window. When he reached her, again in the soft and friendly voice he told the dog to stay. Marcus set the knife on the table reached down to her wrist and untaped her wrist. Again, he could hear her, "Mmmmm." He began to remove the tape over her mouth when she shouted to him in a terrified voice, "He's in the kitchen!"

Marcus jumped to his right as soon as he heard Sam yell. The momentary flash from the rifle when Dave shot at where he believed Marcus to be was enough to point out where exactly in the dining room the doorway to the house interior was. Keeping low, Marcus made a mad dash for it. As he moved he heard Dave eject the spent rifle cartridge and a new one was inserted into the rifle.

Dave took the flashlight out of his pocket, turned it on and he focused it on Tripper. The light moved so that it lit up the hallway leading from the dining room. Marcus could not be seen. Dave moved the light back to the dog and he talked to it, "You okay? You good enough to get him?" Dave reached out and patted the dog. "Come on boy. You can tear the mother fucker apart." Tripper got up and trotted to where Dave stood. Dave shined the light on the still bound woman, didn't notice that her right wrist was untaped, and he said, "You stay put." The two walked to the hallway. As he walked in that direction he continued to talk and encourage the dog. "He can't get out. We'll get him Tripper," and the dog jumped a step ahead of Dave. The talk to the dog made him enthusiastic about the hunt. When Dave reached the hallway, he turned on the overhead light to reveal that there were three doors off the hallway. When he reached the first doorway he held the flashlight under his arm and twisted the knob. He took the flashlight in his hand and pushed the door open with his rifle and pointed the gun into the room. He commanded the dog to wait and the dog waited. A quick look inside with the flashlight showed nothing so he reached around the corner and flipped the light switch on. He pushed the door all the way open until he heard it hit the door stop against the floorboard. "You in here?" he asked. "Get him Tripper!" and the dog bounded into the bathroom. Dave followed and pulled the shower curtain aside. "Not behind the shower curtain. Let's go boy."

They reached the second door on the opposite side of the hallway across from the bathroom door. Again, Dave opened it the same way he did the bathroom door to reveal it was a bedroom. The dog stayed behind him until he turned on the room's lights and he then told the dog to sic him. Tripper ran around Dave into the room and showed a bit more enthusiasm about the hunt. Running around the room the dog sniffed. Nothing. Dave stepped into the room and quickly shined the flashlight and looked under the bed, no one there. Dave then opened the closet door. The flashlight showed there was no one in the closet.

Dave and the dog reached the last door at the end of the hallway, the master bedroom. He slowly twisted the doorknob, held the flashlight in one hand and again pushed the door open with the rifle. A quick scan of the room with the flashlight Dave was holding as he stood in the doorway showed nothing. He reached around the door opening and turned on the light and it was then that he noticed that the window was open. He took a step into the room and cursed under his breath. He spoke to the dog, "He went through the window! He's outside!" Dave turned to the dog to leave and he shouted, "Let's go!" The dog turned and started down the hallway. Before he could follow, Marcus behind the door pushed it closed and pulled Dave back into the room. He then hit Dave before he could recover. When Marcus had hit Dave, he knocked him down and the rifle went flying across the room. Dave quickly got up and swung at Marcus with his flashlight. He missed and Marcus hit him with his right hand and knocked Dave against the wall. Dave came right back at Marcus and this time he also held the knife that he had in a sheath on his belt. He swung at Marcus' face again with the flashlight. Marcus saw the blow coming and instincitly turned to his right and lifted his left shoulder. The blow knocked Marcus down and it hurt. He scrambled for the rifle. Dave saw what he was trying to do and lunged at Marcus and stabbed down at him. Marcus was able to fend the stab off and then he hit Dave's arm with the knife. It went flying from his hand. Both men now raced to the gun. Before Marcus could reach it, Dave kicked it under the bed. Marcus could reach Dave and grabbed his leg and pulled it out from under him so that Dave was toppled to the floor. Both men got up and continued to fight. Dave was getting the better of Marcus because Marcus could only use his right arm effectively. The flashlight hit he took to his left shoulder pained Marcus when he tried to use it. Dave swung at his opponent's stomach and hit Marcus and he went reeling back. Dave dropped his guard after he hit Marcus and believed Marcus would go down. Instead, Marcus hit him in the stomach and sent him backward toward the bedroom wall. Dave hit the wall, but he did not fall. Marcus rushed to him and tried to grab him in a bear hug as best he could with just one arm. With one arm around Dave, Marcus rushed him against the wall. Dave had his wind knocked out of him when he hit the wall and was momentarily dazed. He slid down the wall until he hit the floor and was sitting on it. Marcus went to the bed and was reaching under it for the rifle. Scratching could be heard on the door. Dave reached up and turned the doorknob and as the door swung open he called out to Tripper, "Get him boy!" Nothing happened and the door swung open further. Dave shouted to the dog, "Sic him boy!" The dog stuck its head through the door but didn't enter.

Marcus stopped trying to get to the rifle for a moment and looked at the dog, expecting it to come bounding across the bed for him. Behind the dog, he saw Sam leaning against the hallway wall, holding a piece of firewood in one hand, the butcher knife he set on the table in the other. He heard her menacingly say, "Stay! Both of you!"

Marcus had retrieved the rifle, laid it on the bed and pointed it at Dave. "Let me see your hands! As you said, this rifle will make a big hole you try anything. Be careful of the dog Sam. Call 911 and get the sheriff, I'll watch Dave Winters and the dog."

She turned to go and said in a commanding voice, "You move dog, you'll lose the other eye." Marcus could hear the dog whimper and saw it cower against a wall. Maybe the dog did understand what people said to it.

Before she left Marcus yelled to her, "Didn't see a phone and if he has one don't know where it is. Use our cell in the car. Stay outside until the sheriff arrives," and he heard her open and close the front door. He kept the rifle pointed at Dave for what Marcus believed was twenty minutes when he heard a police car siren. From what he could see of the dining room he saw the red flashing lights of the police cars on the wall.

Shortly the house was swarming with police officers. When they came into the bedroom, they handcuffed Dave, took the rifle from Marcus, and helped him up. Marcus had re-hurt his left shoulder and now he had trouble moving his arm. A policeman escorted him out as soon as Dave had been removed from the bedroom. Outside in the driveway Marcus saw four police cars and an EMT van. An officer placed the hand cuffed Dave Winters in the rear of his cruiser. Sam was at Sheriff Tillman's car and she was talking to him. The policeman guided Marcus to them, and the questions began. When he complained about his shoulder the EMT helped him remove his jacket and shirt and began to examine his neck and shoulder. Marcus couldn't see the left side of his neck and shoulder but he could feel the blood running down his chest. As the EMT worked on the wounds that had opened when he was hit with the flashlight. Marcus told the sheriff all that he knew about Dave and what he had done. Sheriff Tillman told an officer near him to take a couple more men and search Dave's house.

When the emergency medical technician finished working, Sam asked, "Is he okay?"

"It appears the collar bone is cracked," the technician replied, "and his previous wound was torn open and bleeding a little. I've stabilized the arm and shoulder and it will need to be fixed at the hospital."

"I'm so glad you're okay Marcus," she said to him and held his hand. She turned and looked at the sheriff and asked, "What about his dog?"

The sheriff answered, "One of my men got a restraining leash on him Ma'am, and I've already put a call in to animal control. They will send someone out to take care of it and the puppies you told us about." He looked at Marcus and said, "Tomorrow I'll have our CSI go over his house for any evidence we might find that will tie him to the murder of the treasury agent, not just your word. Finding the money would help. My men are doing a preliminary search right now."

Marcus said to the sheriff, "If what he told me about hitting the agent with a piece of wood was true, it might still be in the rear of his truck and possibly would show traces of blood or hair."

From the house the front door opened and one of the officers sent to search came through the door holding a metal suitcase in his latex gloved hand. He walked to Sheriff Tillman and said he found it on a top shelf of the closet in the bedroom. "Is this what you are looking for?" he asked.

"It sure looks like it," Marcus said. "Have you opened it?"

"No, thought the sheriff should do it," the officer replied.

Sheriff Tillman told the officer to set it on the hood of his car, he then put on his own latex gloves and released the two latches and opened the lid. Everyone near the sheriff just stared as a policeman shined his light into the case. The officer near Marcus holding the flashlight gave out a short whistle and said, "I've never seen so much money at one time before."

When everyone had seen the money, the sheriff closed the suitcase and handed the suitcase to the officer that had found it and said, "It better all be there when it reaches the station."

Marcus could hear a faint, "Yes sir, it will be," as the officer walked away.

Sheriff Tillman said, "Agent Larson will be glad to hear that it's been recovered and we have the guy who killed her agent. I'll tell her in the morning.

Chapter 15

The next morning the sheriff had a deputy drive Marcus and Samantha in a jeep out to the lake where Agent Larson had divers searching the water. The road where it washed out had been replaced recently for all the treasury searchers. It was a bit rough going over the area usually washed away, but the jeep made it fine. When the jeep arrived at the base camp Agent Larson approached it and greeted Sam and Marcus. "You two didn't need to come out here. Sheriff said your shoulder is still banged up and I see your arm's in a sling again. He said you found the guy who killed Agent Turner too. Quite a day for you two."

Samantha asked, "You having any luck?"

"No, but we did find Agent Beale's gun in the lake. We're on the right track," Ms. Larson said to her.

Marcus heard what she said and shook his head no. "You won't find any money in the lake," he said to her. "I don't think it's there."

"Why do you say that after you already found a suitcase full of it there? How do you know?" Ms. Larson asked.

"I don't know for sure, but I do know where I would look," he replied.

"I'm listening," the treasury agent said.

Two days later Sam, Marcus and Cory Larson were looking at the prospector Ellery's mine entrance. Inside the mine men were working on clearing the cave-in and re-shored up the ceiling and sides. "On a hunch that you are correct I've hired a half dozen miners to clear it out and keep it from caving again," Agent Larson said to Marcus.

Marcus heard her and replied, "It's the only possibility that hasn't been checked."

"You could be right Marcus. What made you come to that conclusion?" Sam asked him.

"When Dave Winters was threatening to kill me, he said he'd bury me so deep in one of the abandoned mine shafts around here, I'd never be found," he replied. "I remembered that I had seen a pack saddle on the mule when Ellery found us at the plane crash. Saw it again on a rail under his lean-to for his mule and that waitress in the restaurant explained exactly what the pack saddle was and how it was used. He had come to the crash not knowing what had happened, but he was prepared to pack back to his cabin anything he might find of value. Reason for all the rope he had. That prospector was so familiar with the area he could have found the wreckage at night in the blizzard. He could have packed all the suitcases on his mule and taken them to his cabin. Question he had to answer, where could he hide all the suitcases where they wouldn't be found, and he was sure they would be looked for. In his mine was the answer. But what would prevent treasury agents from searching it?"

"A cave in!" Sam replied. "But he got killed."

"Yes, he did, that part was not planned on. He decided to cave in his mine and come back years later and dig it out," was Marcus' answer.

"He just didn't get out in time," Ms. Larson said.

"No, he didn't. Question for you Agent Larson, was an autopsy done on Agent Beale when he was taken out of here?" Marcus asked.

"Not that I know of," she answered. "It was assumed that he died of exposure."

Sam said, "Ellery could easily have smothered him after everyone was asleep, slip out and return to the crash."

"All that you two are saying is possible, I'll run it by my boss and see if he wants to pursue it," Ms. Larson said. After a moment of silence, she added, "If you are right about where the money is, in the mine, there's going to be a big finder's fee."

Two days later Sam and Marcus were back at the site. "It's been almost three days now. Much more of the mine caved in than first believed," Ms. Larson said to Sam and Marcus. "But it's cheaper to hire miners than scuba divers. Heard from Sheriff Tillman that Dave Winters finally confessed to killing Agent Turner but claims it was in self-defense. He tried to steal the money from Winters."

Marcus said he heard the same thing from the sheriff and said, "Only time will tell if that strategy will fly. Means I'll most likely have to come back to Twin Pines it goes to trial."

A miner came out of the mine and reported that they were past the cave-in. Now they were going to search deeper into the mine. He returned to the mine when Ms. Larson said, "Here's hoping." It wasn't five minutes later when the same miner emerged from the mine, carrying a metal aluminum suitcase in each hand, and asked, "Is this what you are looking for?"

It was a week later when Sam was driving their rented SUV. She read the inspection stop ahead sign and was slowing down. When she reached the inspection area she stopped and put her window down. A California border inspection guard approached the SUV. "Where you folks coming from?" he asked.

"Colorado," she answered.

"Any fruits or vegetables?" was his next question.

"No, nothing," she answered him.

His next question was, "Where you heading?"

"San Francisco," she replied and before he could ask anything else, she said, "and home,"

Instead, the inspection guard asked, "Big dog. What kind is he?"

This question was answered by Marcus, "Not sure."

"What happened to his eye?" the inspection guard asked next.

"In a fight, "Sam said.

The guard forgetting where they were going, said what he so often said to visitors as he waved them through, they heard him say, "Enjoy your visit to California," disregarding that she said, "and home."

The End